THE VOYAGE
THROUGH THE IMPOSSIBLE

Borgo Press Books Translated by Frank J. Morlock

Anthony: A Play in Five Acts, by Alexandre Dumas, Père

Falstaff: A Play in Four Acts, by William Shakespeare, John Dennis, William Kendrick, and Frank J. Morlock

Michael Strogoff: A Play in Five Acts, by Adolphe d'Ennery and Jules Verne

Peau de Chagrin: A Play in Five Acts, by Louis Judicis

Shylock, the Merchant of Venice: A Play in Three Acts, by Alfred de Vigny

The Voyage Through the Impossible: A Play in Three Acts, by Adolphe d'Ennery and Jules Verne

William Shakespeare: A Play in Six Acts, by Ferdinand Dugué

THE VOYAGE
THROUGH THE IMPOSSIBLE

A Play in Three Acts

by

ADOLPHE D'ENNERY & JULES VERNE

Translated and Adapted by

FRANK J. MORLOCK

THE BORGO PRESS

An Imprint of Wildside Press LLC

MMIX

CONTENTS

DEDICATION

To Jean-Michel Margot,

For enthusing me with Verne,
And for helping me to obtain this
And other rare Verne texts

CAST OF CHARACTERS

(There is no character list in the French text)

In order of appearance:

EVA
MADAME DE TRAVENTHAL
TARTELET
GEORGE
NIELS
DOCTOR OX
MASTER VOLSIUS
THE FALLEN ANGEL
HOTELIER
VALDEMAR
AN ENGLISHMAN
AN OFFICER
CAPTAIN ANDERSON
A JEWELER
1st HINDOO
ANEMON
ELECTRA
CELENA

ACT I

SCENE I

THE CHATEAU D'ANDERNAK

(A great hall of a castle of Danish Saxon architecture. To the right, an organ whose side is leaning against the wall. Night is falling. Madame De Traventhal is seated busy with work on a tapestry. Eva is at a table looking at maps and books which she leafs through.)

EVA: Here they are then, the travel books, these maps that our poor George peruses ceaselessly. The pages are covered with notes—which show how much they trouble his mind! Look, grandmother! Crayon marks everywhere made by a feverish hand! These voyagers have discovered the most distant parts of our globe! They risked their lives to visit them, from one pole to the other! And that would not suffice his ambition! On this margin, the words "Forward! Much further! Yet further still!" Alas, never! George will never recover peace of mind.

MME DE TRAVENTHAL: Eva, my dear girl, you mustn't despair: George loves you, he knows he's loved by you! He's never known any family than ours since the misfortune which struck down his father whose reason was lost in his ambitious enterprises. But soon it will be twenty years that George has lived with us, at Castle Andernak. Our care will end by moderating his exalted imagination. He will understand that happiness is here, in family life, and God will make him remain.

EVA: Let's hope so, grandmother, let's hope so.

MME DE TRAVENTHAL: But it's my concern that he remain unaware of the blood he was born to.

EVA: Son of Captain Hatteras whose audacity led him almost to the North Pole, and who, alas, came to die in a lunatic asylum. Oh, you are right, he must never know—his already overly exalted mind could experience a fatal seizure.

MME DE TRAVETHAL: The poor child. Where is he right now? How did he pass the night?

EVA: Still very agitated. Our old Nils told me he walked for a long time in his room. He uttered incoherent words and those words which sum up all his thoughts. "Forward! Much further still!" What is to be done? Couldn't we consult a doctor?

MME DE TRAVENTHAL: I've already thought of that. But so as not to expose our concerns to George on this subject, the doctor will come for me.

EVA: For you?

MME DE TRAVENTHAL: I am expecting his visit this very morning. I had him summoned by that good Mr. Tartelet.

EVA: By Mr. Tartelet?

MME DE TRAVENTHAL: Who seemed completely delighted that we really wanted to use him for something.

EVA: I understand him. This brave man came from Paris without recommendations and without resources—presenting himself as a dancing master.

MME DE TRAVENTHAL: Yes, professor of dance and deportment.

EVA: You received him, or rather sheltered him, and as no one here has the heart to dance—

MME DE TRAVENTHAL: He's remained among us in the character of a friend.

EVA: But a very uneasy, quite tormented friend, my mother.

MME DE TRAVENTHAL: Why?

EVA: Because his delicacy is alarmed by stipends that he

receives without any profit from his lessons

MME DE TRAVENTHAL: Fine! Isn't he now almost one of the family?

(Tartelet enters by a side door)

TARTELET: It is I, ladies.

MME DE TRAVENTHAL: Ah—Mr. Tartelet—Well?

TARTELET: The celebrated doctor will be here in a moment.

MME DE TRAVENTHAL: A thousand thanks, Mr. Tartelet.

TARTERLET: And—with that, Madame?

MME DE TRAVENTHAL: (astonished) With that—what?

TARTELET: Wouldn't you have some little thing for me to do, madame?

EVA: For you to do, Mr. Tartelet?

TARTELET: Yes, Miss, yes. You mustn't think I am useful only for jumping capers and scraping the violin. An old bachelor like me, forced to care for himself has to know many little skills. I know how to repair damaged furniture, glue precious crockery, sew buttons back on.

If needed, I can even do washing.

EVA: (laughing) You do washing, Mr. Tartelet?

TARTELET: Yes, Miss, but unfortunately, I don't know about ironing.

MME DE TRAVENTHAL: Don't trouble your mind, my good Mr. Tartelet; we know that you love us and (offering him her hand) that suffices for us.

TARTELET: It suffices for you, it suffices for you, Madame, but it doesn't suffice for me. Every morning I present myself at the hour of my lesson—and—I never give my lesson. And still you pay me.

EVA: Well, if I am not disposed to take it?

TARTELET: Then, Miss, I ought not to be disposed to take the fee, I've lived in the castle for six months—which comes, by reason of one lesson a day, to 180 lessons that I have not given. Which, at two shillings each, comes to a total of 360 shillings that I have received and that I am going to have the honor to return to Madame. (pulling his purse from his pocket)

EVA: Will you put that away, naughty man!

MME DE TRAVENTHAL: I thought that you considered yourself our friend?

TARTELET: Me, your friend! It's a great honor, madame.

I would be happy to, but—I don't want to be a friend at two shillings a day.

MME DE TRAVENTHAL: It's an account on which we will have to pay you much later.

TARTELET: Much later? I don't understand.

MADAME DE TRAVENTHAL: Well, for your future students

TARTELET: My future students? I still don't understand

MME DE TRAVENTHAL: It's really very simple. You know that George and Eva are fiancés. They will marry one day or the other—soon, perhaps. And—in the future (low) Can't you grasp?—a whole class of pretty little students.

TARTELET: Ah! yes, yes. I see, I get it! To take young children from their earliest age, to show them how to place their pretty little feet from the moment they come into the world. To develop their childish grace. What joy, what happiness, what a dream!

MME DE TRAVENTHAL: It will be realized, Mr. Tartelet. You see quite well you cannot leave us. What would you do besides? You would return to give private lessons in Paris.

TARTELET: In Paris? Oh, no, Madame, no! They don't dance there, they leap and that's all.

EVA: They leap?

TARTELET: Yes, Miss, yes. And not only in the salons, they leap in the Bank, on the Exchange. They leap about everywhere. We even have clever choreographers who make prefects and ministers jump—and who are famous dancers themselves.

MME DE TRAVENTHAL: What are you telling us there?

EVA: So dancing is no longer practiced in Paris?

TARTELET: In Paris, Miss, in Paris, they only know the dance of money.

EVA: Hush—here's George.

(George enters from the left, pensive, somber, without seeing anyone. He goes to sit at the table and mechanically leafs through the open books in front of his eyes.)

EVA: (aside) Oh! My poor friend!

MME DE TRAVENTHAL: You are right; he's more depressed than ever.

GRORGE: (hands on the maps) They penetrated there—these extraordinary heroes. Into the bowels of the earth, under seas, across space! Lidenbrook, Nemo, Ardan—there, where no one had set foot before them! And this other one, Captain Hatteras, the Conqueror of the North Pole, towards whom I don't know what strange sympathy attracts me most keenly. And I, who feel in myself the strength to equal them, to surpass them, perhaps, I have done nothing yet, nothing! (he remains depressed, head in hands)

EVA: (coming to him) Your hand is burning, George.

GEORGE: (raising his head) It's you, Eva. (to Madame de Traventhal) It's you, mother.

MME DE TRAVENTHAL: Are you ill, George?

GEORGE: Yes. It's like an incessant fever consuming me. Against which all human remedy will be impotent.

EVA: Not even friendship?

MME DE TRAVENTHAL: (pointing to Eva) Not even—love?

GEORGE: Eva! (going to her) My darling Eva, I love you, you know that. My heart belongs to you. It's yours, too, mother. But my imagination is stronger than my heart! Each hour of the day or night it takes me far from the castle, far from this country—beyond terrestrial boundaries, almost into worlds unknown. And I hear a voice which calls me: Forward—further still—yet further still1

EVA: Calm yourself, George, I beg you. Ah, if you really loved me.

GEORGE: I love you Eva. Our two beings will be made one—someday. But only after the realization of my dreams. Now, I cannot belong to you completely. I feel it. I shall go first where my destiny leads me.

TARTELET: And you will need famous legs to follow it.

EVA: (taking his hand) So you are thinking of abandoning us.

GEORGE: I will come back to you, Eva.

EVA: And if you can no longer find me on your return?

GEORGE: No longer find you. What do you mean?

EVA: I don't know but it seems to me that a danger threatens me.

GEORGE: A danger? What danger?

MME DE TRAVENTHAL: What is it, daughter? Speak!

EVA: For some time, whenever I leave the castle accompanied by old Nils, I am followed by a man whose presence causes me real terror.

GEORGE: Who is this man?

EVA: I don't know. But he's a creature of strange allures—bizarre—which frighten me. You would say he knows in advance what I am going to do and where I am going to go.

GEORGE: And you say he follows you everywhere?

EVA: Everywhere. And, strange circumstance, he stops only when I enter into the Church. In the doorway of Saint-Lieu. His glance becomes even more strange, A bitter irony contracts his lips and the fire of rage shines in his eyes.

GEORGE: And when you've gone into the church?

EVA: Calm returns to my soul. Especially when it's Master Volsius who is playing the organ.

GEORGE: Master Volsius?

EVA: Yes, the new organist, attached, I believe, to the Cathedral of Aalbourg. An artist of genius; I almost said a superhuman artist! For when he accompanies the penitential psalms, the depths of Hell open before your eyes! When he sings the glories of the Almighty, it's really to Paradise that he transports you. Then, and as if by a marvelous enchantment, the walls fall away, the church disappears, and it's a celestial vision he invokes in the midst of the most divine harmonies.

MME DE TRAVENTHAL: Yes, Eva, yes! I, like you, have experienced these sensations listening to him.

EVA: It's more than ecstasy. You see— What this great artist wishes to express: you see it, mother, you really see it.

TARTELET: And I too, I've seen, yes sir, yes. I've seen this prodigy. And they assure me that this man is not only an organist without equal. He can extract the most miraculous effects from my violin. He can make houses dance.

NIELS: (entering) Madame, the doctor is here—

GEORGE: (excitedly) A doctor?

MME DE TRAVENTHAL: Yes, children, a doctor I've had brought for me. They informed me there was at this moment in Aalbourg a doctor of great reknown. I had him asked to come. He will give me some good advice. To you also, Eva, and you, George, and Mr. Tartelet.

TARTELET: But I am not ill.

MME DE TRAVENTHAL: One is always ill—more or less. I've noticed doctors cure especially—

TARTELET: —especially when one is feeling well.

MME DE TRAVENTHAL: Show in Doctor Ox.

GEORGE: The Doctor Ox—who made such extraordinary experiments in doubling vital faculties under the influence of oxygen?

MME DE TRAVENTHAL: The same!

GEORGE: I am curious to see him.

TARTELET: (aside) Mr. George doesn't need an oxygen supplement; rather, he needs to be kept away from it a little.

NIELS: (announcing) Doctor Ox.

(Ox enters by the door at the back)

EVA: (aside, with terror) What have I seen. Him! The man who ceaselessly stalks me.

DOCTOR OX: (to Madame de Traventhal) You had me called, madame. Here I am.

MME DE TRAVENTHAL: Doctor, I learned of your presence in Aalbourg where your great reputation has preceded you, and I decided to consult you.

DOCTOR OX: For this young girl, perhaps?

EVA: (excitedly) For me? No, no.

MME DE TRAVENTHAL: Are you really sure of that? Look at this pallor, this agitation. (grasping her hand)

EVA: Ah!

DOCTOR OX: And this hand; so frail that it shakes in mine. (Eva pulls her hand back, he holds it.) It's like fear, terror even. We will calm this.

EVA: (getting away from him) You are mistaken. I am neither afraid nor terrified. (aside) My forebodings tell me that with this man, misfortune has entered our house.

GEORGE: (to Doctor Ox) Doctor, I am happy to know you. I have followed your experiments from a distance but with profound interest.

DOCTOR OX: Truly?

GEORGE: To increase the proportion of oxygen in the air, to transform the body and the soul. To double, triple the vital faculties. That is magnificent!

DOCTOR OX: Yet simple, sir. The human body is like a lighted stove! I found quite easily the way to put in a bit more coal. But let's talk straight, sir. It's you I must treat here.

GEORGE: Me.

MME DE TRAVENTHAL: Doctor, what are you saying?

DOCTOR OX: No vain beating around the bush, Madame. The health of this young man is dear to you?

MME DE TRAVENTHAL: Very dear, yes; without a doubt.

DOCTOR OX: And to you also, Miss?

EVA: (frigidly) George is my fiancé, sir.

DOCTOR OX: (aside) Your fiancé. (aloud) So—his mind nourishes dreams which appear to you foolish, and you wish to cure him of great ideas which bubble in his brain.

GEORGE: So then; it's for me they made you come.

DOCTOR OX: For you. For you alone.

MME DE TRAVENTHAL: Who told you that, sir?

DOCTOR OX: In these parts, Madame, your name is known to everyone. And the story of this young man is known to all but him alone.

GEORGE: What's he say?

DOCTOR OX: You are counting on me to effect his cure! Well, so be it. I will undertake that cure. But do not expect me to deflect his thoughts from the glorious goal he has long pursued.

EVA: What?

DOCTOR OX: Do you understand what may happen in compressing gas to prevent it from exploding? No, no! Let him expand. On the contrary, his generous ardor— Don't stop his noble exaltations. Let him say what he wants to attain, and let's try to pave the way for him.

GEORGE: What I want, Doctor, is to do more than the heroes whose names are written in these books have done. To go beyond the boundaries they could not cross.— Professor Lidenbrook who thrust himself into the bowels of the earth.... As for me, I want to go to the fiery core. Captain Nemo, prisoner of his *Nautilus*, searched for independence under the sea. As for me, I want to live in that element and scour it from one pole to the other. The audacious Michel Ardan shut himself in a cannon shell to go gravitate a few thousand leagues from earth. As for me, I want to run from one planet to the next. That's what I want, Doctor! Is it so impossible?

DOCTOR OX: (in a powerful voice) No!

EVA: Sir, what are you daring to say?

DOCTOR OX: No, a thousand times, no! What you aspire to, on the contrary, you shall know and your eyes shall see. If your courage doesn't weaken.

GEORGE: I will dare all. Speak! But it's not a question of vain dreams?

DOCTOR OX: It is in reality itself that I will escort you there.

GEORGE: In reality!

DOCTOR OX: (pulling a flask from his pocket) See this flask! Whoever shall drink a few drops of this liqueur will be transported with the rapidity of lightning and in the condition of a new life to places forbidden to man! No more intervals of time. No more intervals of distances. Days turn into seconds, years into minutes.

GEORGE: And I shall go to the fiery core of the earth?

DOCTOR OX: Yes!

GEORGE: And to the bottom of the seas?

DOCTOR OX: Yes!

GEORGE: And wherever I wish in space?

DOCTOR OX: Yes!

GEORGE: Ah! That would indeed really be the impossible.

DOCTOR OX: The impossible which you will accomplish. Because I will give to your body the faculty not to burn when others burn, of not to drown when others drown, of breathing when there is no air to breathe. And, after having been transported as in a vortex, you will return a hero from the impossible, having penetrated the most unfathomable mysteries of Nature.

EVA: Such an attempt is not only foolish, George, it is evil, it is sacrilegious.

MME DE TRAVENTHAL: (terrified) Yes, my daughter,

you're right. In the name of Heaven, sir, not another word.

GEORGE: Leave me alone, leave me alone, mother! Doctor, I believe in you and I am ready to follow you.

EVA: George you will be abandoning us! She who nurtured you, loved you like her child. And me, George.

DOCTOR OX: (forcefully) Go: pray, weep, soften his heart, weaken his soul, and turn back into infancy this son of Hatteras that I was going to make into a man.

MME DE TRAVENTHAL: (to Eva) Great God!

GEORGE: (forcefully) Son of Hatteras, did you say? I am the son of Hatteras, the son of the audacious navigator who raised himself to the North Pole?

DOCTOR OX: Yes, yes. This illustrious man was your father!

GEORGE: My father. He whose marvelous exploits I devoured! He whom I wanted to equal.

DOCTOR OX: And you will surpass him if you wish.

GEORGE: Ah, from now on nothing will stop me.

MME DE TRAVENTHAL: Alas, all is lost.

EVA: This man is the evil genius of our family.

DOCTOR OX: (aside) Now, he is mine.

MASTER VOLIUS: (entering) Pardon, ladies and gentlemen. Am I really here in the home of Madame de Traventhal?

MME DE TRAVENTHAL: Yes, sir. May I know—?

VOLSIUS: Madame, leaving the Cathedral, I by chance found this book of hours, and thinking it belonged to someone at the Castle, I took the liberty—It is yours, perhaps, Madame?

MME DE TRAVENTHAL: No.

VOLSIUS: (to Ox) To this gentleman then? Yes, it must belong to this gentleman.

DOCTOR OX: (recoiling) To me?

VOLSIUS: Take it. Why, take it then, sir?

DOCTOR OX: (still recoiling) This book, mine? No, no, I tell you!

VOLSIUS: Oh! Don't be afraid; it won't burn your fingers!

EVA: (coming forward) It's my book of hours that I forgot this morning at church. And I thank you for having returned it to me.

DOCTOR OX: Who are you really, sir?

VOLSIUS: I, sir? I am the organist at the Cathedral.

EVA: Master Volsius!

ALL: Master Volsius!

GEORGE: Volsius: the great artist.

VOLSIUS: Volsius the humble organist, sir.

OX: (aside) What's he come to do here?

EVA: Ah! Sir! How many times have we heard you at the Cathedral! How many times have we been thrilled by the sublimity of your harmonies.

VOLSIUS: Miss, I am only a poor artist.

MME DE TRAVENTHAL: To whom Castle Andernak will always be open.

DOCTOR OX: (aside) We shall see about that.

MME DE TRAVENTHAL: (presenting) My granddaughter, Eva—

VOLSIUS: Miss.

MME DE TRAVENTHAL: (presenting) Her fiancé, George

GEORGE: (sharply) George Hatteras.

VOLSIUS: Son of the celebrated Captain Hatteras.

GEORGE: (very animated) Yes! Yes! He's my father. My father, who I am going to equal, to surpass his discoveries. Thanks to the wise Doctor Ox.

VOLSIUS: (turning towards Ox) The Doctor Ox! I have heard much said of Doctor Ox. Are you well, Doctor Ox?

DOCTOR OX: (turning his back on him) Very well— Master Volsius.

VOLSIUS: They say doctor that you possess the ability to give the human body the power to go through the impossible.

DOCTOR OX: And they say the truth, Master Volsius.

VOLSIUS: And to discover mysteries the knowledge of which God seems to be reserving to himself alone?

DOCTOR OX: Yes. We will penetrate those impenetrable mysteries.

VOLSIUS: And you are offering to the son of Captain Hatteras to undertake, on his own account, those attempts that came to ruin even in mythology? To renew the experiments of Icarus?

DOCTOR OX: Yes. And without breaking his wings.

VOLSIUS: The adventures of Prometheus?

DOCTOR OX: Yes. Without risking the vulture's talons.

VOLSIUS: And the works of the Titans?

DOCTOR OX: Yes, and without fear of being struck by Jupiter's lightning.

VOLSIUS: Why, truly, you have great fortitude!

TARTELET: (aside) Heavens, why it's the organist. He seems to me to be the deepest.

DOCTOR OX: I think, Master Volsius, that you are mocking the power of this liqueur! Well, drink a few drops and you will no longer be in doubt.

VOLSIUS: Thanks, Doctor. I don't need any.

GEORGE: (trying to seize the flask) Then to me! Mine!

VOLSIUS: (holding him back by his arm) Young man, the vain attempts that I've just mentioned have not been able to touch your soul; no one indeed believes in the reality of these mythological fictions. But open these holy books and you will find the proudest ambition, the most audacious rebellion, the most dreadful punishments! And these are so real, these are so terrible, that Doctor Ox himself would dread to confront them.

DOCTOR OX: (with fury) What punishments? Speak, reply!

VOLSIUS: (sweetly) Pardon, a thousand pardons, doctor. I wasn't expressing myself. I wasn't speaking well. They say that—in the end. I am going to try to make myself understood with my fingers. (going to the organ and sitting at the keyboard) I am going to show you in what a profound abyss sacrilegious pride is engulfed.

DOCTOR OX: What's he going to do?

EVA: Lord, inspire him. Save George. Lord, Lord—Save us all!

(The organ resounds)

SCENE II

(The back of the room opens up. The sides disappear and the set represents the fall of an angel. Ox at first recoils, then he returns and looks.)

DOCTOR OX: It's the fall of an angel.

VOLSIUS: It's the punishment of pride.

DOCTOR OX: You are a marvelous artist, Master Volsius. But the fallen angel is gloriously fallen. The grandeur of his fall has made his name almost as illustrious as his audacious rebellion. He has conquered glory and glory before all else!

GEORGE: Yes, yes. Glory, glory!

DOCTOR OX: That's where I will take you.

VOLSIUS: Yes. To glory or to folly.

MME DE TRAVENTHAL: Folly!

VOLSIUS: But he will find me everywhere on his way. (he leaves with Madame de Traventhal)

DOCTOR OX: Come on, George Hatteras. Take this flask and drink. (George drinks)

EVA: (tearing the flask from him) Well, George, I won't abandon you. I will share these perils. (she drinks in her turn and hurls the flask away)

GEORGE: Eva! What have you done?

DOCTOR OX: She, too! Well so be it!

TARTELET: (picking up the flask) What? With this liqueur they can? (drinking) Let's go then.

BLACKOUT

SCENE III

(The terrace of an Italian inn with hills covered with vines. To the right the osteria with doors and windows. In the rear, to the left the whole landscape of Vesuvius. The crater is pouring out smoke. To the right extends the bay of Naples. It is early morning.)

TARTELET: Where are we, anyway? I don't see the town of Aalbourg anymore, or the towers of the Cathedral.

GEORGE: (to Doctor Ox) Where are we, doctor?

DOCTOR OX: At Naples. Not far from Vesuvius whose summit you can see,

GEORGE: Vesuvius? Yes, it's through this crater that Professor Lidenbrook left again.

DOCTOR OX: And it's through this crater that we will penetrate to the center of our sphere.

EVA: To the flaming lake! George, there is still time to stop.

GEORGE: Fear nothing, Eva!

TARTELET: Heavens. It seems to me, I am hungry. One doesn't travel 600 leagues without having a bit to eat.

DOCTOR OX: Here's an inn! Call: they will serve you. Meanwhile, we will go to prepare for the perilous descent.

TARTELET: Preparations? What for? Since with a single jump you can cross hundreds of leagues.

DOCTOR OX: (to George) Is it a question of simply reaching the goal without having seen anything, understood anything, studied anything?

GEORGE: Surely, no.

DOCTOR OX: Do you wish to avoid all the perils, be unaware of all the secrets, all the mysteries?

GEORGE: No, no.

DOCTOR OX: Then come along.

TARTELET: Go on. You'll find me here. (the others leave) Eh! Fine! Now let's call. Hola! Waiter!

HOTELIER: (enters, looking at those who are leaving) Heavens—a traveler.

TARTELET: Why, yes. Come forward, waiter. That seems to surprise you.

HOTELIER: Sir, it surprises me greatly!

TARTELET: Then you are alone here, waiter?

HOTELIER: Alone with a Dane who arrived yesterday.

TARTELET: A Dane. I knew a really handsome one. With superb ears and a long muzzle. It was a pretty dog.

HOTELIER: Why, no. This one here's a young man.

TARTELET: Ah, great; a two-footed Dane. Waiter, tell me; what have you got for me?

HOTELIER: Not a thing right now; the Dane ate everything.

TARTELET: That's okay. Give me any old thing. And not overdone.

HOTELIER: Right away, sir. (he leaves)

VALDEMAR: (enters and bows to Tartelet) Ah! I ate well! Perhaps I ate a bit too well.

TARTELET: It's the Dane; he doesn't have a long muzzle!

VALDEMAR: Heavens, a foreigner. Sir.

TARTELET: (bowing to him) Sir. (aside) What a gauche figure. He doesn't even know how to bow properly.

VALDEMAR: Hello, sir! Sir—sir—customarily, when traveling when one meets at the end of the earth or even not so far—one easily makes acquaintances. Dare I ask who you are?

TARTELET: Professor Tartelet.

VALDEMAR: (aside) A professor! He's a scientist. (aloud) From what country, sir?

TARTELET: I am French. Born in Asnières.

VALDEMAR: Asnières. Ah! Right. Asnières de Bigorre, I know—

TARTELET: Why, no.

VALDEMAR: You are married, Mr. Tartelet?

TARTELET: No. Why such a question?

VALDEMAR: Then you don't have any little Tart-lets?

TARTELET: No

VALDEMAR: (laughing) No little Tart-lets?

TARTELET: No Tartelets. (aside) What kind of over-grown child is this? (looking at Valdemar's feet) Oh, such feet.

VALDEMAR: You were saying?

TARTELET: Out, young man, further apart.

VALDEMAR: (astonished) Further apart? He's asking me to leave. He wants to be alone. (starts to leave)

TARTELET: Why, where are you going?

VALDEMAR: You told me, "Apart."

TARTELET: Why, yes, I was referring to your feet. That's what we call a choreographic angle.

VALDEMAR: Huh?

TARTELET: (touching him with the end of his cane) A bit more separated—wider—wider (Valdemar almost falls) That's very good like that.

VALDEMAR: Oh, you like that do you? What a funny scientist.

TARTELET: I have the honor of speaking to Mr...?

VALDEMAR: Axel Valdemar—of Copenhagen.

TARTELET: Marvelous; eh—well, Mr. Axel Valdimar.

VALDEMAR: No, pardon me, Valdemar.

TARTELET: Right! Right!

VALDEMAR: And you are coming—?

TARTELET: From Aalbourg.

VALDEMAR: By train?

TARTELET: No

VALDEMAR: By boat?

TARTELET: No.

VALDEMAR: By stage coach?

TARTELET: No—running.

VALDEMAR: Running?

TARTELET: A running current. Electric.

VALDEMAR: An electric current?

TARTELET: Yes!

VALDEMAR: And you are going?

TARTELET: (pointing to the ground) There.

VALDEMAR: Into a cave?

TARTELET: Down further?

VALDEMAR: Down further? They're listening to us.

TARTELET: Under the earth. To the center of the earth.

VALDEMAR: To the center of the earth.

TARTELET: Through the crater!

VALDEMAR: Not possible!

TARTELET: Not possible. But we are going to do it. My friend, your feet. (correcting his position)

VALDEMAR: Again! What a funny scientist. What a funny scientist.

TARTELET: And you, Mr. Vladimir?

VALDEMAR: Val-de-mar, *s'il vous plait*.

TARTELET: Right. Confidence for confidence. Where are you going to, Mr. Vladimir?

VALDEMAR: (aside) He's keeping it up. (aloud) Mr.— Mr. Tartelet. I am going to a place where one can make one's fortune.

TARTELET: I don't know yet where that place is.

VALDEMAR: You conceive that I love a charming young girl from Copenhagen, Miss Babichok.

TARTELET: And naturally, Miss Babichok doesn't love you, Mr. Vladimir?

VALDEMAR: Valdimir again! But I tell you my name is Valdemar.

TARTELET: Ah, pardon me, young man. It's one of those names I'll never learn to pronounce, and I feel I'll never be able to say it, Wait. I prefer to call you Mathew. Is that agreeable?

VALDEMAR: Mathew is okay with me. I once knew a Mathew very well.

TARTELET: Me, too.

VALDEMAR: He was an astronomer.

TARTELET: Mathew Laensberg; then you were saying, Valdemar.

VALDEMAR: Ah! Great! There now, you said it.

TARTELET: Ah, pardon me. I am mistaken. You were saying that Babichok—

VALDEMAR: —is madly in love with me. Ah, what a woman! What soul! What heart! And pretty. When I think of her I have palpitations. You know palpitations.

TARTELET: Do I know palpitations? We have big ones and small ones.

VALDEMAR: (astonished) Big and small?

TARTELET: Which allows one to raise one leg and move it from low to high, while the other leg supports the entire weight of the body.

VALDEMAR: Can I try? What?

TARTELET: Palpitations—like this (does one) Try.

VALDEMAR: (aside) He is ill! (aloud) Why, that's not the kind of palpitation I was speaking of. What a funny scientist!

TARTELET: I wonder why, since she adores you, you haven't married Babichok?

VALDEMAR: There are two obstacles to our union. First of all, Babichok finds me too fat and too thin.

TARTELET: What do you mean?

VALDEMAR: Too fat, personally—and too thin in my fortune.

TARTELET: Ah!

VALDEMAR: Eh! Well, yes, I am a little bit chubby. I said to her. But the more one has of what one loves the better. Also, as to plumpness, perhaps she ought to yield, being much too thin herself. The two of us would have made a good average. An interlarded family.

TARTELET: Yes. That was self adjusting. Nothing more remained then but—

VALDEMAR: But the fortune! But, impossible to give her up. She loves me too much! "My Valdemar," she said, "I want you to be rich, very rich. So you can have a pretty carriage, fine horses. A beautiful mansion where I can adore my idol at my ease. But to see you in discomfort, in misery, you, oh! I would suffer too much from that; and I would prefer to try another than to have the misery of sharing your poverty." Is that true love or what? Tell me, Mr. Tartelet.

TARTELET: That's perfect love. Grade A quality.

VALDEMAR: So, I left in the hope of making a fortune and of developing, through traveling, the brilliant aspects of my soul.

TARTELET: You did well, Mathew. Your feet.

VALDEMAR: I've already seen some not-bad countries, and profitably, I dare say. I have studied the mores. I have observed the customs, and I've noted down all my poetic impressions in this notebook.

TARTELET: That must be curious.

VALDEMAR: See, here. France—admirable country. Paris, admirable country.

TARTELET: That's brief, but it's plain to the point.

VALDEMAR: I have to make myself understood. At Paris, ate calf and lamb. Switzerland.

TARTELET: Swiss lamb?

VALDEMAR: No, that's not it. Switzerland, admirable country! Geneva, admirable country. Ate lamb chops and veal. Italy: Rome! Rome—

TARTELET: Ate veal, beef and lamb.

VALDEMAR: No. I let you say that from politeness. There isn't any. There you only eat goat, just as here there is only macaroni.

TARTELET: You are writing all these impressions for Miss Babichok?

VALDEMAR: Naturally! This will distract her as will cousin Finderup who I left with her.

TARTELET: Ah! There's a cousin, Finderup?

VALDEMAR: Yes. A friend of mine. A fine lad whose fortune I shall make and who writes me everywhere I stop and gives me news of my fiancée.

TARTELET: Well, is it done?

VALDEMAR: No, not yet! But I don't despair. I will succeed! For her, you see, I shall attempt the impossible.

TARTELET: The impossible? That's exactly where we are going. Are you coming with us?

VALDEMAR: Where's that?

TARTELET: Down under.

VALDEMAR: In the cave, again?

TARTELET: In the center of the earth.

VALDEMAR: What to do?

TARTELET: Why, to make a fortune there. Isn't the general stash of expensive things there? Money, gold, diamonds? Isn't it from the bowels of the earth that one extracts the most precious things in the world?

VALDEMAR: That's true indeed. It's the general cash box! All you have to do is fetch it up. But I don't have the key.

TARTELET: But we have it.

VALDEMAR: And you will lead me there?

TARTELET: Yes, if you'll consent to drink a few drops of a certain liqueur which will transport you there in a few seconds?

VALDEMAR: —running current?

TARTELET: Electric.

VALDEMAR: But this liqueur?

TARTELET: I have the flask! And if I drank it inadvertently you will drink it from ambition.

VALDEMAR: Ah! Mr. Tartelet. What luck to have met you? A drop—only a little drop?

TARTELET: Yes, but on one condition.

VALDEMAR: I accept in advance.

TARTELET: It's that for two hours a day you will place your feet in the third position.

VALDEMAR: What is this thing you call the third position?

TARTELET: Look. Like this.

VALDEMAR: (astonished but obeying) Like this. Gladly. But why do you want me to put my feet in the third position, you, a Professor?

TARTELET: Of dancing, my friend.

VALDEMAR: Of dancing! And I took you for a scientist.

TARTELET: Come drink a drop of the liqueur in question!

VALDEMAR: Yes, yes,—a drop. Let's drink a drop. (they leave; the George, Doctor Ox, and Eva enter)

GEORGE: Everything is ready. And if there are some dangers to run, you won't tremble?

EVA: Surely not!

DOCTOR OX: (to George) You wish to leave—

GEORGE: Right away. The crater of Vesuvius is there: open to the audacious who are not afraid to descend. Were it to shut over us: little matter! Let's go.

DOCTOR OX: Ah, indeed! Yes, to the center of the earth.

(Volsius enters disguised as Professor Lidenbrook)

VOLSIUS: To the center of the earth! ah! ah! ah! Those are big words, very sonorous and pretentious. To go there seems to me a real folly.

GEORGE: Sir, to whom have we the honor of speaking?

VOLSIUS: Professor Lidenbrook.

GEORGE: The Professor Lidenbrook who went—?

VOLSIUS: —about a hundred leagues under the Earth and not more. Because it was impossible to go any further. And if you find me at Naples within sight of Vesuvius, it's because I returned to the surface thrust up by an eruption of lava. The place seemed beautiful to me and I decided to stay here for a while.

DOCTOR OX: Ah. Professor, you declare it impossible to cross limits that you yourself were unable to cross.

VOLSIUS: (laughing) Right, sir, right.

GEORGE: Is it then forbidden to reach glory by means of a road others have been unable to follow?

VOLSIUS: Ah! That road is all laid out, sir, parallel to the mouth of Vesuvius, that you see smoking from here; there is another which will lead you where I went if your heart tells you so.

DOCTOR OX: We must go beyond that.

VOLSIUS (laughing) Beyond that? Ha, ha, ha!

GEORGE: And we will go beyond it.

VOLSIUS: But, gentlemen, I stopped when it was no longer possible to go further.

DOCTOR OX: (ironically) When you didn't dare go further?

VOLSIUS: You think so! My word, gentlemen, you are very brave; your bold attempt transports me! And you make me want to begin this trip again with you.

GEORGE: Nothing prevents you.

EVA: Yes! Yes, come, come, sir. I don't know why but your presence reassures me.

VOLSIUS: (hesitating) Well, it's decided. You intend to go to—

DOCTOR OX: To the center of the Earth.

VOLSIUS: I don't know why you are risking yourselves

in such endeavors, but I will be your guide and go with you.

DOCTOR OX: Then are you coming?

EVA: George, in the name of Heaven!

VOLSIUS: (aside to Eva) Let him do it, miss. There are limits in the face of which they will really be forced to recognize the importance of humanity; and they won't cross them. Come, my child, come.

(all leave.)

BLACKOUT

SCENE IV

A HUNDRED LEAGUES BENEATH THE EARTH

(The stage represents an immense crypt with depths and openings in all directions. Stalactites hang everywhere. Rocks in the rear allowing descent to the floor of this natural catacomb.)

TARTELET: (appearing) Come on, young Valdemar.

VALDEMAR: (issuing from the height of the rocks) Here I am! Here I am!

TARTELET: The Devil! The road is not kind to the legs of a dancer. (to Valdemar) Watch out you don't break your ankle.

VALDEMAR: Don't worry.

DOCTOR OX: Come on, George Hatteras. Further, even further.

GEORGE: I am following you, doctor. This is the abyss, and the abyss attracts. I will go on to its final depths. (they begin to descend)

VOLSIUS: (to Eva) Don't be afraid, my child; the danger has not yet come.

EVA: (afraid) I'm not worried for myself, but only for him.

VOLSIUS: It's at this point we are going to rest.

GEORGE: Where are we?

VOLSIUS: Why, in my home.

DOCTOR OX: Indeed. I think here is the limit of your voyage, Doctor Lidenbrook.

VOLSIUS: And if this can interest you, I will tell you that these hollows stretch under Central Europe, under France and right under Paris—the place we are now.

VALDEMAR: Under Paris! The Paris that I visited and loved is above my head, and one cannot hear the noise of the great city! (some distant rumbling is heard) Eh! Indeed! You would say a great roll of carriages; we must be beneath a crossroads of the throng.

EVA: (to Volsius) But those rumblings!

VOLSIUS: A rumbling which produces itself at intervals in the structure of the Earth.

VALDEMAR: An earthquake: Let's get out of here. (he leaves)

DOCTOR OX: Well, George Hatteras, what do you think of these immensities which stretch to infinity under the oceans, under the continents, and which support cities and mountains? Did you expect to find here a subterranean vegetation where the humblest plants of the earth become trees under the influence of a hot and humid environment? And that this air, become luminous from pressure, would light these silent catacombs?

VOLSIUS: Doesn't the contemplation of these marvels suffice to satisfy your ambition as an explorer?

GEORGE: What use would be the new vital power given to our bodies by Doctor Ox, if it only was a question of going where others had gone before us, or where you yourself had gone? What's here is extraordinary, but not the Impossible.

DOCTOR OX: (aside) Fine! Fine! (A great scream is heard off)

EVA: What was that?

TARTLET: That's Valdemar's voice!

VALDEMAR: (reentering, terrified) Ah, I found you again.

TARTELET: What happened?

VALDEMAR: (pointing to a stone) This stone; do you see this stone?

TARTELET: An odd stone.

VALDEMAR: It's not ordinary. So I am keeping it. But what is extraordinary indeed is the strength with which it landed on my back.

TARTELET: Landed? By what?

VALDEMAR: By what? That's what I ask you? There are lots here and heavy. Come see how heavy it is for its size.

VOLSIUS: Everything is heavy here, young man.

VALDEMAR: What do you mean everything is heavy here?

DOCTOR OX: No question! It's the natural result of attraction.

VALDEMAR: Attraction?

VOLSIUS: And if we get to the center, your billfold will become so heavy as to split your pocket.

VALDEMAR: My billfold—heavy to that degree. Now there's a thing that astonishes me.

DOCTOR OX: That's not all. Acoustics even are modified in this environment where the air is submitted to an enormous pressure.

GEORGE: So that noise, sound will take on an immense intensity?

TARTELET: Heaven's, it's true. The scream that young Valdemar uttered just now resembled a roar.

VALDEMAR: A roar?

TARTELET: Why, then my dance master's violin will have quite a different sonority.

VOLSIUS: Try it.

TARTELET: Right away. (taking his violin and playing a gavotte with a surprising power of tone)

VOLSIUS: That's prodigious.

TARTELET: It's admirable. Let's continue.

(As Tartelet plays the heads of strange creatures appear amongst the rocks at the back, listening and exchanging signs of the most extreme surprise; faces very flat, expressions very savage, hair disordered)

EVA: (noticing them, screaming) Ah! Look at those monsters.

GEORGE: (turning towards the rear) Great God!

EVA: George! George! stop!

(Tartelet stops playing; the monsters disappear.)

DOCTOR OX: Yes—stay—Besides, you see, they've disappeared.

GEORGE: What are these strange beings?

DOCTOR OX: This is the first of the mysteries which have been revealed to us. There exist in the subterranean depths an entire race of living beings.

GEORGE: An entire race!

VALDEMAR: An entire race!

TARTELET: —of living beings! Well, we will instruct them in the first principles of the dance.

VALDEMAR: Perhaps one of these gentlemen threw this stone at me!

GEORGE: But how could a human race be able to form in these depths and live here?

VOLSIUS: Ask that of the wise Doctor Ox.

DOCTOR OX: Nothing could be simpler! It suffices that in one of the upheavals of nature which have taken place over millions of years—it suffices that some of the inhabitants of the earth were engulfed here. They populated these vast solitudes, and their descendants changed, little by little by the place in which they lived, ceased to resemble the human race and degenerated as you just saw.

VALDEMAR: Come—

EVA: It seemed just now that music exercises a kind of fascination over them.

VOLSIUS: Yes, that's true.

GEORGE: What's become of them? Let's look for them.

EVA: No, no!

DOCTOR OX: What is important to discover now is the path by which we will reach our goal.

GEORGE: (as a great subterranean noise is heard) Hear those noises which circulate through the earth's shell.

VALDEMAR: It's having convulsions at the moment.

DOCTOR OX: And soon, perhaps, the fire will open the way for us that communicates with the earth from Vesuvius's crater.

VOLSIUS: And you would dare proceed that way?

GEORGE: Yes, yes!

DOCTOR OX: We dare to do it!

VOLSIUS: But I repeat to you, this is more than boldness, this is—

DOCTOR OX: Quite simply, this is courage. Do you understand courage, Professor Lidenbrook?

VOLSIUS: Go where your pride leads you. (to Eva) I will pray ardent prayers for you, poor child; you who are resignation, virtue, piety. (to Doctor Ox) Piety and virtue, do you understand that, Doctor Ox? (he leaves)

EVA: He's going away.

DOCTOR OX: Let him leave! Deliver us from his cowardly remonstrances. (a new, more powerful noise) Listen,—hear that again! It's coming from the direction which will open the path we are seeking.

GEORGE: Come. We will find it together.

EVA: George. (Doctor Ox and George leave.) George!

VALDEMAR: The other one seems more prudent to me. I am going to try to catch up with him. (leaving by the other side)

EVA: Alas, he no longer hears my voice.

TARTELET: It was a bad idea your grandmother had to summon this cursed doctor to the castle!

EVA: My friend, he would have come sooner or later.

TARTELET: What do you mean?

EVA: Sooner or later he would have seized George's imagination; not to calm him, nor cure him, but to ruin him.

TARTELET: And for what purpose?

EVA: That's the man who's been stalking me.

TARTELET: Him. Ah, I understand. He dares to love you. Ah, if I could manage it, Doctor Ox, what a pretty dance this dancing master would teach you.

EVA: Don't you attack him, my friend! He's gifted with a strange supernatural power. (Doctor Ox appears at the back) Everything about him terrifies me! The imperious power of his voice; the irresistible fascination of his glance. (Doctor Ox comes slowly toward Tartelet.)

TARTELET: The fact is—in his eyes, I recognize a diabolical expression.

EVA: Him!

TARTELET: (noticing Doctor Ox who looks him in the face) A diabolic—no, I, I, mean— (Doctor Ox takes his arm and gestures for him to leave)

DOCTOR OX: Leave us.

EVA: Stay here, Mr. Tartelet.

DOCTOR OX: (looking at Tartelet square in the face, more imperious still) Obey!

EVA: No—no—

DOCTOR OX: Leave. I wish it.

TARTELET: What's the matter with me? I try vainly—I cannot; I cannot— (Tartelet backs away despite himself)

EVA: (calling) George! George!

DOCTOR OX: George is far from here and cannot hear you.

EVA: I know quite well how to get him back! (calling) George!

DOCTOR OX: (barring her way) I must speak to you!

Eva—do you know why, a while ago, I followed you everywhere? Why I wandered around your dwelling?

EVA: I don't want to know!

DOCTOR OX: Why? I love you.

EVA: (with irony) You love me? You!

DOCTOR OX: If I came to Castle Andernak it was neither for your grandmother nor for your fiancé, George. It was for you, for you alone! I wanted to be near you, to see you, to listen to you—because I love you.

EVA: Enough! Not another word.

DOCTOR OX: And do you know why I revealed to George the name of his father? Why I pushed him on this path? Why I gave him the power to accomplish all his desires? Because I didn't want George to become your spouse. (forcefully) And because I love you.

EVA: When George learns what your plans are and why you are urging him towards this impossible world, reason will return to him, and he will kick you out like an evil genius that has finally been unmasked.

DOCTOR OX: Eva, you will be silent. To speak would place us face to face like two rivals, and you know quite well that the struggle would be more dreadful for him than for me.

EVA: I will speak.

DOCTOR OX: You will kill him then. I will no longer have a reason to lead him to folly. You will have brought him to death.

EVA: My God, George, George! This man will kill you.

DOCTOR OX: Understand me, Eva! I love you! I love you.

EVA: Ah, don't profane that word! Threaten me! I much prefer your rage to your threats!

DOCTOR OX: Well—so be it! No more vain prayers. But remember my last words. Soon, you yourself will come to beg my pity for this George. You will beg me to stop him from pursuing his path. You will ask me mercy for his sanity, for his life. But it will be too late (going)

EVA: Pity! Pity for him—

DOCTOR OX: It will be too late. (he is gone)

EVA: (coming forward, lost, broken) My God! What to do? What will happen? He will kill him. Ah, my strength abandons me. I can't do any more. I feel I am dying. (calling) George! George! George!

(Her voice weakens and she falls senseless. At this moment from all sides, the subterranean inhabitants of this region appear behind the rocks. They advance furtively.

One of them, their chief, guides them to the middle of the stage. The savages approach Eva and look at her with keen surprise. They lean over her. The chief kneels, raises her head, parts her hair, touches her face and her hands; looking about him he makes a sign to his companions to keep away. He lifts her up and is going to carry her away. Eva comes to, then, noticing the monsters around her she utters a terrified scream.)

EVA: Ah! (trying to free herself, but the chief holds her) Help! (struggling the chief raises her in his arms and rushes toward the rear of the stage. George enters running from the left.)

GEORGE: Those screams (noticing Eva in the hands of the savages) Ah! Eva!

EVA: Help! Help!

GEORGE: I'll save you, Eva. I will save you or I will die with you. (rushes the chief but he is seized and thrown to the ground. Doctor Ox returns from the right followed by Valdemar and Volsius. Tartelet comes in from the left.)

TARTELET: Ah! My God.

VALDEMAR: Those horrible monsters.

DOCTOR OX: (coldly) They are lost. (the savages turn towards them, then throttle George and Eva.)

GEORGE AND EVA: Ah!

GEORGE: Save her—her, save Eva!

TARTELET: Let's run!

VOLSIUS: Silence! (seizing the violin Tartelet carries)

DOCTOR OX: But her, Eva!

VOLSIUS: Don't anybody move! (making the violin vibrate with sounds of strange intensity. The savages stop, listen, and seem fascinated. Volsius keeps playing. The Chief lets Eva fall. He listens more closely. He puts his head close to the instrument; his companions approach, too—crawling as if chained to Volsius' bow. Volsius moves away and the savages end by disappearing led away by Volsius, while the song of the violin makes itself heard in the distance.)

GEORGE: (running to Eva and taking her in his arms) Ah! Eva—darling, Eva!

EVA: Let's leave this cursed place. Take me away, take me away, I beg you.

VALDEMAR: Ah, yes. Let's get out of here.

TARTELET: Ah, Master Lidenbrook; what a man; I could never have played like that.

VALDEMAR: My friend, my good friend, trust me. Let's

get out of here.

GEORGE: Yes, yes, they're right. Let's turn back on our steps. Eva, I intend to take you far from here. I never intended to expose you to such perils. Let's leave.

DOCTOR OX: Leave? When at any moment the obstacle which keeps us from our goal will perhaps collapse.

GEORGE: What are you saying?

EVA: Don't listen to this man, George, don't listen to him. (rumblings)

DOCTOR OX: There. Listen, look. It's the Earth opening up again. Look, look, George Hatteras! It's the first rung of your fame, of your glory. The first crossing of the impossible.

BLACKOUT

SCENE V

THE FIERY CORE

(The stage represents the center of the Earth. Flames everywhere, jets of sparkling fire, incandescent lava spreading everywhere. Torrents of liquid metals, silver and gold, fusing together.)

DOCTOR OX: Well! Now do you believe in the power I've given you? And do you promise to follow me henceforth?

GEORGE: Everywhere, Doctor! Wherever you wish to lead me.

EVA: (aside) He's lost to me.

GEORGE: (running across the stage looking at everything distractedly) Yes, yes, indeed: this is the incandescent center of the Earth. Fire everywhere, everywhere. I breathe it in long bursts. And what a new existence, and what indomitable strength is manifesting itself in me. Fire—it's the soul of nature, it's universal life, and my blood, heated by it, boils in my head and circulates in my veins like torrents of lava.

DOCTOR OX: (with irony) Fine! Fine!

GEORGE: It electrifies my soul. It unveils to my dazzled eyes mysteries unknown to man.

DOCTOR OX: (to Eva, pointing to George) Hear him! see him!

GEORGE: No. You are not vain and fabulous fictions, marvelous dwellers in fire! Appear phoenix, *Ignus fatuus*, and salamanders! I will proclaim to the world the reality of your existence. For I've seen you! I see you! I see you!

(Phoenixes, salamanders, and *Ignus fatuii* appear. They dance a ballet.)

DOCTOR OX: (returning toward the end of the ballet, and leading George to center stage) Son of Hatteras! You have conquered Professor Lidenbrook. Next, come eclipse the glory of Captain Nemo!

(They vanish in the midst of dancers who perform their last dances.)

CURTAIN

ACT II

SCENE VI

(The stage represents a plaza on the roadstead in Goa. To the right, the city on rising ground with its mosques and its Hindu houses; its villas are lost in the trees. To the left, a hotel with a veranda and awning. To the right, a jeweler's shop. In the rear, a roadstead with ships, fishing sloops and further back, a merchant vessel with its sails half unfurled and sporting an English flag. It is broad daylight. A crowd comes and goes on the plaza whose extremity is cut off by a balustrade forming a quay on the roadstead. The crowd is composed of men and children, Hindus, porters, sailors; among them, Captain Anderson, an Englishman, and a jeweler.)

FIRST HINDU: Well, has this terrible monster reappeared?

JEWELER: Not yet; but if it returns I wouldn't give a sequin for all the ships in the roadstead of Goa.

FIRST HINDU: Decidedly, the Indian Sea is no longer safe; and I pity the ship which adventures into our ports.

SHOUTS IN THE CROWD: There it is! There it is!

FIRST HINDU: Why, no; it's only a reflection of the Sun on the horizon.

(The crowd, very agitated, moves toward the parts of the plaza adjoining the roadstead.)

JEWELER: The terrible animal will cause me some harm! Ships will no longer dare to adventure into the roadstead of Goa. No more ships, no more travelers. What will become of commerce in jewelry and precious stones?

ENGLISHMAN: (to Captain) This marine monster has really turned several people's head, Captain?

OFFICER: First of all, is it indeed a marine monster?

ANDERSON: And what do you want it to be? A great number of navigators have observed it and several ships attacked by it have had trouble to escape it. It is even possible we may owe it the disappearance of several ships of which we've had no news.

OFFICER: Ah, don't deny the catastrophe's due to the presence of a powerful being that for several years past has shown itself on the surface of the sea—one day in the Atlantic, the next in the Indies, for it seems to be endowed with a prodigious faculty of locomotion.

ANDERSON: It's a real danger for navigation. But I notice down there some passengers I'm negotiating with. You'll allow me?

OFFICER: Go ahead! Go ahead, Captain. (Anderson moves away)

VALDEMAR: (alone, emerging from an inn) Bon voyage, gentlemen! Ah, it's the depths of the sea they intend to go visit now. Well, I won't follow them. I went with them right to the center of the Earth. That's great. I came back; that's better. I've had enough of it, not to mention that I've found nothing in the face or the sod. I only brought back (pulling a pebble from his pocket) this stone that I received in my back. I won't carry it around any further. (tossing it to the ground; it unintentionally strikes the foot of the jeweler who leaves his shop.)

JEWELER: Yi! What was that?

VALDEMAR: Excuse me, sir—it's a stone I let fall.

JEWELER: (vexed) Ah! sir, a stone, a stone.

VALDEMAR: Heavens, yes. It's really a curious enough stone that I brought back from the center of the Earth. (showing it to him)

JEWELER: From the center of the Earth! What are you saying! (looking at the stone, aside) Eh! Why—I'm not mistaken. This stone—is it possible? It's a—yes—it's a (aloud) precious stone.

VALDEMAR: Precious! If you think it is worth something, what would you give me for it?

JEWELER: I would give, I would give—200 sequins! Does that suit you?

VALDEMAR: (astonished and laughing) Two hundred sequins for this? Ha, ha, ha, ha!

JEWELER: Do you accept?

VALDEMAR: (laughing) You're making fun of me. Come on. Two hundred sequins for this stone?

JEWELER: (aside) He knows what it's worth. (aloud) Well—yes—my offer is—

VALDEMAR: A joke.

JEWELER: A simple joke, it's true.

VALDEMAR: That's what I said.

JEWELER: And to speak seriously, I offer you 10,000 sequins.

VALDEMAR: (getting angry) Ten thousand! Ah! why you are making even more fun of me, sir, and I won't put up with it.

JEWELER: Pardon, pardon Milord. Don't get carried away. I see that you know perfectly well what your diamond is worth, and I am ready to give it to you.

VALDEMAR: (taking back the diamond) Huh? What? You say my—

JEWELER: Your raw diamond.

VALDEMAR: (very moved) My diamond. My raw—my diamond? It's a diamond and still raw. Look, look, let's understand each other. You swear this is really a diamond?

JEWELER: You didn't know it?

VALDEMAR: Me? Why, not on your life!

JEWELER: (with energy) He didn't know it!

VALDEMAR: It's you who just taught me. (shaking his hand) Thanks, honest jeweler, thanks. It's—a diamond! A diamond you would buy for consideration?

JEWELER: For consideration of 500,000 sequins. Are we in agreement?

VALDEMAR: It's a diamond, and what a huge one. A diamond for which you offer 500,000 sequins and which, consequently, is worth a million at least (dancing and singing)

JEWELER: Are you giving up selling it?

VALDEMAR: Not at all! I will sell it, I will sell it in Europe, in France.

JEWELER: In France!

VALDEMAR: And my fortune will be made. And what a fortune. Ah, dear Babichok, my faithful fiancée who is awaiting me there with Cousin Finderup. I am going to marry you, by proxy, through my cousin—by telegraph. And you are going to be happy…you will no longer fear my being poor. And Cousin Finderup, he's going to be happy! Rich—I am rolling in it. (dancing and singing) Ah, if Tartelet could see me—with my feet out. Ah, what joy, what luck.

JEWELER: (aside) Why, he's going to lose his head.

VALDEMAR: My friend—is there a telegraph in this town?

JEWELER: Yes. With the wire from Europe.

VALDEMAR: And one can send a dispatch?

JEWELER: No doubt!

VALDEMAR And by paying ten times, a 100 times the price of the dispatch one would have an immediate response?

JEWELER: That's likely.

VAL:DEMAR: Ah! Babichok, dear Babichok. Millionaire. Seventeen times a millionaire! You will have carriages, castles, a cashmere from India. (to Jeweler) In India they must have cashmeres from India?

JEWELER: Admirable ones! They come from Paris.

VALDEMAR: I'll buy nine of them. The telegraph? Where is the telegraph?

JEWELER: (aside) He's gone mad!

VALDEMAR: (to Anderson who enters) If you please, sir—the telegraph?

ANDERSON: Down that way—to the right.

VALDEMAR: Thanks, sir. I am going to telegraph my luck to Babichok. (leaves running)

JEWELER: I missed a great deal. (going back into his shop)

DOCTOR OX: (leaving the hotel followed by George, Tartelet and Eva) Well, sir, is everything prepared to receive us on your ship?

ANDERSON: Yes, sir.

GEORGE: (feverishly) And are going to leave? Leave most rapidly, reach the open sea, and once arrived there, Doctor—Ah! Ah!

DOCTOR OX: (low) Silence!

ANDERSON: My ship is an excellent sailor, gentlemen. And I'll do my best to land you in Valparaiso in less than six weeks.

GEORGE: To Valparaiso—us? Ah! ah! ah!

EVA: (watching him uneasily) George!

DOCTOR OX: It's not at Valparaiso we will leave your ship, sir.

ANDERSON: But I am going directly from Goa to the American coast, gentlemen. And, unless you wish to disembark on the high seas—

DOCTOR OX: Who knows? On the high seas, perhaps—

GEORGE: On the high seas! Yes, that is the path we must follow. To plunge across the waves. To reach the bottom of the abyss.

EVA: George, you frighten me.

GEORGE: (coming to himself) Eva, dear Eva, reassure yourself. You will not confront these perils. I don't want that.

EVA: Me? Separate from you? Never!

ANDERSON: I am going to have some singular passengers.

TARTELET: (who, having mixed with the crowd comes downstage) What are these fine folks talking about? They pretend that a marine monster is parading in the waters of their roadstead.

DOCTOR OX: (laughing) A monster.

ANDERSON: Don't laugh, gentlemen. There really is a formidable creature that has been wandering for a month in the Indian waters.

DOCTOR OX: (laughing) A monster?

GEORGE: So much the better!

ANDERSON: You say so!

GEORGE: We will combat it, Captain.

DOCTOR OX: Some fanciful octopus, some legendary Kraken.

ANDERSON: No, it's a sort of whale; a phosphorescent monster of a length of about 250 feet whose passage produces a terrifying backward eddy, and which leaves a blazing white track behind it.

CROWD: (shouting) There it is! There it is!

ANDERSON: Wait; they are doubtless seeing it right now.

GEORGE: Come on, Run!

(All three run toward the quay at the back in the midst of the crowd.)

TARTELET: Alas! The exaltation of poor Mr. George keeps increasing and, thanks to its incredible power the domination that Doctor Ox exercises over him is only too justified. Here we are abandoned to our very selves. (looking around him) By the way! And young Valdemar? Where is he?

(Eva goes toward the back to join George. Valdemar enters from the left.)

VALDEMAR: Ah! Mr. Tartelet! My good Mr. Tartelet.

TARTELET: What's wrong there, young Valdemar?

VALDEMAR: What's wrong? What is it? Hold on—I can hardly speak any more I am so upset. Impossible to say a word. I am too emotional.

TARTELET: Yes, and when you are emotional your feet turn in. Look will you. Look, those feet.

VALDEMAR: We really need stupidities like that now!

TARTELET: (wounded) Huh? Stupidities!

VALDEMAR: Later on—whatever you wish. Lessons by you at ten sous a lesson. A hundred francs, a thousand francs a lesson!

TARTELET: Why, he left his reason at the molten core! His brain is fried!

VALDEMAR: No, it's not fried, but it prances, it leaps, it leaps— Can you imagine that stone I took in the back—

TARTELET: Well?

VALDEMAR: A diamond! A diamond worth millions.

TARTELET: Not possible!

VALDEMAR: They offered me 500,000 sequins for it— here.

TARTELET: Five hundred thousand sequins here!

VALDEMAR: Yes, my good Mr. Tartelet! I am a millionaire! That is to say, we are millionaires.

TARTELET: We are millionaires, you say? "We," you said, "we." Ah, my friend! My good friend, you really said "we," right?

VALDEMAR: Certainly we are millionaires. Miss Babichok and I.

TARTELET: Ah! Miss Babichok that's fair indeed. All my compliments, Vladimir. Ah, this time, she will marry you.

VALDEMAR: If she marries me? She'll do it two for one. Thus, I just expedited a dispatch to Copenhagen announcing my fortune to her and I am awaiting her reply. Can you imagine what her reply will be?

TARTELET: Yes, surely I can imagine. So you are going to leave us?

VALDEMAR: Yes, but as for me, I am not an egoist. I love you, Tartelet.

TARTELET: Thanks.

VALDEMAR: I will beautify the end of your life, Tartelet. When you get old, you will come end your days in our home. In our castle. Tartelet, it will be a palace.

TARTELET: Old? Why, I am, my friend, I am.

VALDEMAR: Oh, no. You're not old enough yet, Tartelet. It's your last, last days I want to beautify.

TARTELET: (aside) He's dumb, but he's got a good heart. (aloud) This Dear Mathew—feet pointed out my friend. Feet pointed out.

VALDEMAR: Yes, professor, yes. Ah, but no! I am rich, I am. I have the right to have my feet pointed in. Hold it; here's how I am going to walk in the future. (struts with his feet pointed in) And I'll make it fashionable. I am rich, and henceforth I will cling to my rank. That's the fashion; the real fashion.

(A small craft has pulled into the quay. It can hold seven or eight passengers.)

ANDERSON: Embark! Embark! (George and Ox get on board.)

TARTELET: Goodbye, young Valdemar.

VALDEMAR: Goodbye, goodbye, my dear professor. (as Tartelet goes to embark, an employee brings in a dispatch)

EMPLOYEE: Mr. Valdemar? A dispatch for Mr. Valdemar.

VALDEMAR: That's me! That's me! It's the reply from my adored Babichok.

TARTELET: Her reply.

VALDEMAR: (reading) "Dear Valdemar! Be happy...." (spoken) Oh, yes, I am, I am. (reading) "...without me. I just got married."

TARTELET: You are saying—

VALDEMAR: (reading) "...without me. I just got married." (spoken) I don't understand.

TARTELET: Let's see.

ANDERSON: Come, gentlemen, come—

TARTELET: Here! Here!

VALDEMAR: (with rage) Ah! The wretch! I'll never see her again.

TARTELET: Believe me, Valdemar—forget the unfaithful one and come with us.

VALDEMAR: Well—well, yes, I am leaving. And she will see what a hero she has lost in me.

ANDERSON: Come, gentlemen.

(Both embark)

BLACKOUT/curtain

SCENE VII

THE PLATFORM OF THE *NAUTILUS*

(Night on the open sea, lit by moonlight.)

DOCTOR OX: (alone, standing on the platform) It's here, under my feet; this formidable monster that spread terror amongst the inhabitants of Goa. It's the ship, the submarine of Captain Nemo, whose reknown my rival, my enemy aspires to eclipse. Patience, George, patience. I will keep all my promises. I will fulfill your most ardent wishes. And it won't be from you that I will demand the price for services rendered. It's she, she whose image is never absent from my sight, the thought

of her fills my entire soul. Eva! Eva! She's there—
beside him. They've been sheltering here like me, after
the shock of the collision threw us on this platform.
Come, let's find her. Come; finish my work.

(He stamps his foot on the deck of the ship. An opening
appears through which he descends. The *Nautilus* disappears, then returns to the stage and opens to reveal the interior chamber.)

SCENE VIII

(The interior of the *Nautilus*. A room elegantly furnished,
lit by an electric light. Divans on each side. In the back all
the machinery. Exterior sides of the *Nautilus* [which is entirely submerged] can be seen. In the rear, doors giving
access to the machinery.)

GEORGE: What a strange and mysterious ship.

DOCTOR OX: It can plunge to the bottom of the sea at
will or travel on the surface. It navigates without the aid
of sails or steam and solely through the power of elec-
tricity.

GEORGE: Doubtless it is armed with a formidable ram,
because when our ship tried to bar its passage, it was
violently lifted up and a big tear was made in the side of
the *Tranquebar* which almost sank it.

EVA: And we sought shelter here. But what has become
of our two traveling companions?

GEORGE: They will have remained on board.

EVA: Or—perhaps they were thrown into the sea.

DOCTOR OX: In that case, they have nothing to worry about, thanks to my precious discovery which permits them to live and breathe in liquid elements.

GEORGE: But what are we doing here ourselves? What is this ship and who is the commander.

VOLSIUS: (appearing as Captain Nemo) You are aboard the *Nautilus*. You are in the power of Captain Nemo.

GEORGE AND EVA: Captain Nemo!

DOCTOR OX: (to George) You wanted to know this hero of the submarine world. You know him now.

VOLSIUS: Are you really sure of knowing me, gentlemen?

GEORGE: We've known your name and your exploits for a long while.

EVA: And we don't expect you plan to treat us as enemies.

GEORGE: And keep us prisoners on your ship.

NAUTILUS: When you know the *Nautilus* better, perhaps you will no longer ask to leave it.

ALL: No longer ask to leave it! Us?

VOLSIUS: Life is a hundred times more peaceable and independent on my ship than it is in your world. Here you need fear neither the Ocean's tempests nor the persecutions of men. Whatever may be the storm raging above, at thirty feet under the waves, it is absolutely calm. Whatever may be the despotism reigning on earth, my *Nautilus* descends to the depths of the waves and I defy all tyrants of the earth. It's one hundred fathoms below the water that one still finds liberty, gentlemen.

DOCTOR OX: Liberty in the middle of a prison.

GEORGE: A liberty of a misanthrope or a savage and not a civilized person.

VOLSIUS: Indeed, gentlemen, I reject that title. No, no—I am not what you call a civilized man. I broke with your society completely. I left your terrestrial soil forever. I exiled myself in good enough company. They've just proscribed God—the so-called God, as they refer to it now.

DOCTOR OX: (with irony) Captain Nemo, is, as I can see, a fervent believer.

VOLSIUS: Very fervent. And more fervent are those who today, as I see it, affect an atheism born of pride or fear.

DOCTOR OX: Of pride or fear, you say?

VOLSIUS: Yes, surely. Proud or timorous. That's what for the most part these pretended atheists are. This group says: if there were a god, would a superior man, a man of genius like me vegetate unaware of it? The others say there is no god, and as to these, it's fear which dictates their language.

ALL: Fear?

VOLSIUS: Eh! Yes, gentlemen, fear. Investigate the lives of these men; rummage in their past; scrutinize their conscience: you will always find some mysteries and somber reason, some shadowy memory which makes them fear a supreme tribunal. They are afraid, I tell you, and if they go everywhere shouting that God doesn't exist, it's at least to make others believe it, in the vain hope of persuading themselves.

DOCTOR OX: (laughing) Ah! ah! ah! It's in the depths of the sea that Captain Nemo wants to reawaken faith and reform our civilization.

VOLSIUS: Ah! Admirable civilization. And on what unshakeable basis does this modern society repose which steals from the disinherited of this world the hope of a better life! But if no other life exists but the terrestrial life, if we must expect neither chastisement nor future reward, virtue is a sham. For crime, the only question is to know cleverly how to escape the law. And because you have at the head of the state some worthy and honest governors practicing a sweet bourgeois philosophy and being pleased to commute the penalties pronounced by justice, you will see criminals emboldened to multiply without release. And murder, no longer being more severely punished than theft, thieves will become murderers and the assassins will say to themselves, "We can kill without fear: they won't kill us! We can strangle without remorse. Remorse is a vain word—for God does not exist!"

GEORGE: Still—what do you pretend to do now?

EVA: Mercy, sir. Don't keep us here. None of us will betray your secret.

VOLSIUS: Well, I am a good prince and I consent that my ship take you where you wish to go.

GEORGE: Why, we are heading toward the conquest of the impossible. Through fire and space.

VOLSIUS: And through water, no doubt. Pour me a few drops of your precious liqueur and I'll leave with you, Doctor Ox.

DOCTOR OX: Ah! You know—

VOLSIUS: Just now through the side of the *Nautilus* your conversation reached me. Yes, I know your name, wise doctor, and your marvelous discovery. I even know who you are, George Hatteras.

GEORGE: George Hatteras, the son of a man who never recoiled before an obstacle and who went—

VOLSIUS: Who went to die—where you yourself are threatening to go.

GEORGE: Stop the lessons, sir; I am not the man to receive them even on your ship.

VOLSIUS: (sadly) You will receive them, alas! and more terrible than mine. You want to leave the *Nautilus* to run about the depths of the oceans. So be it. I told you; I will accompany you.

DOCTOR OX: Even if I don't give you the way to live there where you won't find the elements of life?

VOLSIUS: Even without that.

GEORGE: Well—whenever you wish, sir.

VOLSIUS: Then right now.

(The *Nautilus* shuts and moves away across the waves.)

BLACKOUT/CURTAIN

SCENE IX

SUBMARINE NAVIGATION

(The curtain opened by the *Nautilus* closes little by little then opens to reveal its shape from the rear with its propeller in motion. The *Nautilus* leaves the stage obliquely.)

SCENE X

THE DEPTHS OF THE SEA

(Valdemar, alone. He appears from the right. Bands of fish swim around his feet and disappear through the waves.)

VALDEMAR: This is really the bottom of the sea, and I live, I walk, I breathe in the water as a simple herring would do. What a singular place! The roads here are poorly kept up. But well watered for goodness sake. Not too much sun, either. (looking around) And my companions? What's become of them? It seems to me Tartelet plunged in at the same time as I did. He must have been drawn on further by the current. (schools of fish pass over his head.) Ah—fish—they are flying like birds. Right. There are jellyfish. They look like multi-colored umbrellas! But there are no ladies carrying them from whom I can ask the way. (as he speaks a huge crab moves towards him. Suddenly, he notices it.) A crab! A crab! Ah, the villainous creature! Why, it's me he wants. (fleeing in every direction) Why, I don't know you, I don't know you. He'll end by catching me, the beast! Go—to sleep! (at this moment an enormous shark appears in the upper stratum and descends towards the bottom) And that fish! What a mouth! What teeth! A shark; it's a shark. Help me! Help me! Help! (dismayed, he runs from one side to the other, but the crab is on his heels and the shark approaches opening its formidable jaws) Help!

(He escapes still pursued.)

The scene changes.

BLACKOUT/curtain

SCENE XI

A SUBMARINE FOREST

VALDEMAR: (entering) Whew! I don't want to see those two horrible creatures again. Now where am I? A forest. I didn't expect to meet one under water.
    (stopping in front of an immense oyster) Heavens, an oyster! Ah, ah—beautiful oyster: a dozen like these would make a jolly appetizer for lunch. Suppose I tasted it? Ah, but no—we are in August. It can't be fresh. (at this moment, the gigantic octopus appears; Valdemar notices it.) Ah, my God—Now what's this? An octopus. What? It's after me, too. Why, I am lost. Where to flee. Where to hide? Ah, this oyster, this hospitable oyster. (Valdemar rushes toward the open oyster, he gets in the shell. The two valves close quickly. The octopus disappears.)

TARTELET: (enters looking about carefully. He stops from time to time and calls) Valdemar! Valdemar! (coming forward) Nobody! Still, I saw him jump in the same time as I did. No use calling. (looking on all sides) Nobody. I've been looking for him for a very long while and I am getting very tired. (sitting on the big oyster in which Valdemar is hiding) Let's rest a little. What's become of my companions on this trip? Doctor Ox—I'm not uneasy about that one; but Mr. George and Miss Eva especially. (as he speaks the oyster begins to open little by little.) What a strange effect fatigue is having on me. It seems to me as if the rock I am seated on is rising. (feeling himself raised by the upper valve) Huh? What's under me? I am not mistaken; it really is rising. It's moving. It's rising fast. (trembling) Ah, my God! What is this? (leans on the oyster and it shuts) There's a creature in there. It's rising; it's rising again.

VALDEMAR: (in the half opened oyster) Who's leaning on my shell? Hey—up there!

TARTELET: (trembling) Now it's talking—it's talking!

VALDEMAR: (raising the shell and poking his head out) Tartelet!

TARTELET: It knows my name. It's an oyster of my acquaintance.

VALDEMAR: Why, it's me, Mr. Tartelet.

TARTLET: Valdemar

VALDEMAR: (on his knees in the oyster) Present, Mr. Tartelet.

TARTELET: It was you.

VALDEMAR: Myself.

TARTELET: In an oyster?

VALDEMAR: Why, yes. I didn't find it bad there. I was quite at home. Ah, how happy I am to see you. Everything going well, Mr. Tartelet?

TARTELET: Fine! Fine!

VALDEMAR: And Mr. George? And Miss Eva and Doctor Ox?

TARTELET: I hope we won't be delayed in seeing them again.

VALDEMAR: Let's go. So much the better. But I prefer to see them on terra firma, on dry land as we say in Copenhagen.

TARTELET: Ah—in Copenhagen it's—

VALDEMAR: Dry land, yes, Mr. Tartelet.

TARTELET: But what were you doing in that monster?

VALDEMATR: I was hiding—from a crab.

TARTELET: From a crab?

VALDEMAR: From a shark.

TARTELET: From a shark?

VALDEMAR: And from an enormous octopus.

TARTELET: (gesticulating) From an octopus? Ah, yes, a squid.

VALDEMAR: These three creatures had set out in pursuit of me with suspicious intentions.

TARTELET: What intentions, Valdemar!

VALDEMAR: You see, Tartelet on land men eat fish, and I really think at the bottom of the sea, fish eat men.

TARTELET: You make me uneasy, Valdemar.

VALDEMAR: Ah, I was in a fever of fear. Come! And I'd really like to get out of here and return to the surface.

TARTELET: We'll go back to the surface, but first we must find our traveling companions.

VALDEMAR: Ah! If that ingrate Babichok hadn't married that traitor Finderup I would be in Copenhagen now installed in my house. What am I saying? In my palace. And I'd have my six meals a day.

TARTELET: Six meals?

VALDEMAR: Hell! I had three when I was poor. The least I can do is have six or eight now I am rich.

TARTELET: That's true.

VALDEMAR: My means permit it.

(The tentacle of an octopus sways above the rocks)

TARTELET: Yes, indeed, if your stomach will also permit you— (the tentacle sways over Valdemar's head)

VALDEMAR: My stomach? Ah, I really think it will permit it. Hey! What's that I just felt? (the tentacle coils around his body) Ah! Help me, Tartelet. Help me! (the tentacle drags Valdemar behind the rock) Tartelet! Tartelet!

TARTELET: Ah! Heavens! The unlucky fellow!

VALDEMAR: (reappearing and swaying in the grip of the tentacle) Help. Help! It's choking me. Help.

TARTELET: What to do? Help! Help!

(Tartelet recoils at first in great terror then rushes toward the octopus to tear Valdemar from it, but another tentacle seizes Tartelet who cannot move. George, Volsius, Doctor Ox, and Eva appear at the back. George and Volsius hurl themselves on the monster. Eve, terrified, is thrown to

Tartelet's side. Tartelet gets free and supports her. Doctor Ox joins his companions in attacking the monster with their daggers. At this moment several other octopuses appear and attack the characters. The combat becomes general. The octopi discharge a dark liquid which entirely darkens the water, and it is through this thick fog that one sees the combatants who end by disappearing completely. The fog dissipates and turns into coral grottoes.)

BLACKOUT/CURTAIN

SCENE XII

THE CORAL GROTTO

VALDEMAR: (half fainting, coming to) Where am I?

EVA: In a safe place.

GEORGE: You have nothing to fear.

VALDEMAR: Really, true? Ah, sir, my friends.

VOLSIUS: There you are—completely reassured.

VALDEMAR: (quivering and weeping) Yes, yes. Completely. I want to get out of here! I want to get out of here!

EVA: You were really fearful, Mr. Valdemar—

VALDEMAR: Oh, yes, Miss, oh, yes. I've experienced

numerous fears in my life; I think I may even say without boasting that no one has ever had more frights than I. But frights like this—Ah! never, never. All I ask is to get out of here.

VOLSIUS: But I repeat to you; here under all this pressure, under these coral reefs you are sheltered from all these marine monsters.

VALDEMAR: That's possible. But I prefer to get out of here.

VOLSIUS: I think nothing is keeping you. We've arrived at the lowest depths of the sea.

EVA: And doubtless from here we are going to go back up to the surface.

DOCTOR OX: Go back to the surface? Not yet.

GEORGE: Remain in these marvelous, unknown depths— mysteries which until today have never been penetrated?

VOLSIUS: Never. I attest to that.

DOCTOR OX: And I attest the contrary. All men can get here and live for a short time at least! Here is almost— the possible. But we are still going forward and the impossible shall rise before your eyes; and the past, the irrevocable past itself is going to emerge and recreate itself before your eyes.

ALL: The past?

DOCTOR OX: See those uncertain shapes, those objects which are taking shape in the distant waters—

(Lines vaguely indicating the ruins of an engulfed city appear confusedly)

GEORGE: What is it?

DOCTOR OX: Ask Captain Nemo. He will tell you what it is. He who has often surveyed these seas.

VOLSIUS: That was once Atlantis. The immense continent of Plato, greater than Africa and Asia joined together. And in one day and one night it vanished beneath the sea following some frightful cataclysm.

GEORGE: Atlantis?

DOCTOR OX: Yes, Atlantis where the famous nation of Atlanteans lived. Their domination imposed itself over the entire earth, lending support to the Titans to scale Heaven and kick out the Gods! Well speak. Do you intend to flee at the moment that you can set foot on this continent that no human creature will ever see again?

GEORGE: No, no! But these are only shapeless ruins.

DOCTOR OX: The ruins of Makhimos, one of the most celebrated capitals of Atlantis. It's going to revive for you and return to the ocean's surface.

BLACK OUT/CURTAIN

SCENE XIII

(The city of Makhimos, capital of Atlantis four or five thousand years before the Christian era. The architecture is a mixture of Moorish, Arabic, and Mexican. The water has completely vanished. A splendid sun lights the set. The Atlanteans come and go in the square.)

A HERALD: (shouting) Glory to the gods for inspiring the people to elevate a new king to the throne of Atlantis.

ALL: Glory to the gods.

AMMON: Many days have elapsed since we awaited a successor worthy of King Atlas

ASCALIS: He only left a daughter, Celena, who cannot succeed him to the throne.

AMMON: Celena, the most beautiful of Atlanteans will only be queen after having married the king we have chosen, who must, like that glorious sovereign, brave the lightning of Jupiter to scale the heavens.

HERALD: (shouting) Glory to the gods for inspiring the people to elevate a new king to the throne of Atlantis. (Electra enters)

ALL: The prophetess.

AMMON: What's Electra going to tell us? Has she consulted the oracles? Has she read the future?

ELECTRA: People! Today is the day that the throne vacant through the death of the greatest of kings will again be occupied.

ALL: Ah!

ASCALIS: What mortal will be worthy to succeed him?

ELECTRA: Hear—all: Atlas fell, vanquished by the gods when he lent his support to the Titans revolting against heaven. But the one who is announced to us is more than a mortal. I have consulted the entrails of sacrifices. I have drunk the intoxicating liqueur of laurels; and when I took my seat on the tripod of the Sybylles, a foreign man, born in a distant country, and gifted with supernatural powers appeared before me—

AMMON: Who is this man?

ASCALIS: What mystery has been unveiled? Speak.

ALL: Yes. Speak.

ELECTRA: Listen. He who calls himself the Envoy of Destiny is going to make it known.

ASCALIS: Then let him come.

ALL: Let him come.

ELECTRA: Here he is.

AMMON: Strange, who are you?

DOCTOR OX: I am the messenger of the one your proph-
ecies have foretold, of he who must reign over Atlantis.

ASCALIS: Our race is so degenerate that a man worthy of
the throne cannot be found among us?

DOCTOR OX: When you learn the prodigies accomplished to reach you by the one I represent all your
votes will go to him.

AMMON: Is it a god you are announcing to us?

DOCTOR OX: It is a man whose courage has raised him
completely above mankind. Neither fire nor water nor
terrestrial abysses hold their secrets from him! Who
among the heroes who render your history illustrious
compares to him? Speak! Is there one alone in it who
can be compared to him?

ALL: No, no.

ELECTRA: Let him come and the acclamations of the
people will raise him to supreme power! And he will be
the happy spouse of Celena.

DOCTOR OX: Celena?

ELECTRA: The marvel of Atlantis; the incomparable

daughter of King Atlas.

DOCTOR OX: So let it be done. The one I precede will be the worthy spouse of the daughter of your king. (George and Eva enter) The man you are expecting; he is here.

ALL: Halleluah! Halleluah!

GEORGE: What do they want from me?

DOCTOR OX: They have learned from me the prodigies you have accomplished and their admiration summons you—to the throne of Atlantis.

EVA: What are you saying?

GEORGE: Who? Me? I will be—?

DOCTOR OX: You will be king!

ALL: Yes! Yes!

EVA: Great God!

GEORGE: You've heard! You understand, Eva, you understand! King of this powerful, conquering nation of the past! What honor! What glory! What a triumph!

EVA: (aside) Ah, that's why he led him here. It's the last blow directed against his reason. (aloud) George, listen to me; hear me. Cast aside this illusory monarchy

GEORGE: Illusory, you say—when I am the sovereign of a nation revived for me! For me, who will henceforth unite the marvelous memories of antiquity to glorious modern discoveries! What power is comparable to mine? King of this continent which extends from the ancient to the new world. I am king! I am king!

DOCTOR OX: And this immense nation will prostrate itself before one who has done what no one could ever do again.

GEORGE: (delirious) Yes, yes! Ah! Ah! Ah! Behold at last this glory so much desired; this supremacy so ardently dreamed of! I am the son of Hatteras! I am the King of Atlantis!

EVA: Don't follow the advice of your pride. Shut your ears to these cursed temptations.

ALL: Halleluah! Halleluah!

GEORGE: Listen! Don't you understand the people are acclaiming me?

EVA: This people? Are you forgetting this is only a vain evocation of the past? This country; an ephemeral empire; this monarchy which distracts your imagination. George, my beloved, George, hear my prayer. Take pity on my tears.

GEORGE: Your tears. Why, yes, yes, you are weeping. You Eva! Ah! I won't have you weeping. Do you hear,

I won't have it!

EVA: Then listen to me. Listen to me carefully.

GEORGE: Speak! Speak.

EVA: George, you are heading toward a fateful slope which leads to delirium; which leads to madness.

GEORGE: Delirium? Madness, did you say?

EVA: Yes, yes, believe my word! Have I ever deceived you?

GEORGE: Well yes, I believe in you. And I want—I want to struggle. Speak to me, Eva, speak to me.

EVA: (joyfully) Ah! Our love will save him. Courage, George, courage. Keep fighting. I am at your knees. I, your friend, your sister, your fiancée.

GEORGE: Wait, wait—the shadows are fading. The truth is going to shine before my eyes.

EVA: And you will be saved! George, you will be saved!

DOCTOR OX: (aside) Saved! (aloud) Glory to Your Highness.

ALL: Glory to him! Glory to our King!

GEORGE: (forcefully) Ah! You heard! King! I am really

King!

ELECTRA: Come to the palace that Makhimos erected for its sovereigns. On your return to this square, all the assembled people will crown you with their acclamations.

EVA: No—no. Don't abandon me!

ALL: Glory to him. Glory to him!

GEORGE: Come, come all!

(All leave except Eva and Doctor Ox.)

EVA: (uttering a last cry) Alas! All is lost! (she rushes toward George, but Doctor Ox stops her with a gesture.)

DOCTOR OX: One more such outburst as that, one more blow directed against his reason, his dementia will be complete; his madness incurable.

EVA: Yes. That's where your betrayal will have led him. To ruin him.

DOCTOR OX: Say rather to conquer you, Eva!

EVA: To conquer me!

DOCTOR OX: Isn't his fate in my hands?

EVA: What difference does that make?

DOCTOR OX: Then you no longer fear for him?

EVA: No!

DOCTOR OX: Nor for yourself?

EVA: No.

DOCTOR OX: Then what are you waiting for? What are you still hoping for?

EVA: I am waiting for the most powerful intervention. The succor I am waiting for is for his love to save him—or for him to die.

DOCTOR OX: For him to die! At least I will have separated you from him.

EVA: You are mistaken. If he dies, I shall die with him.

DOCTOR OX: Die for this man who is forgetting you; who never loved you.

EVA: Never loved me, you say?

DOCTOR OX: Never, since he seeks the happiness of his life elsewhere than in you. He had only to extend his hand to seize this happiness and he disdained your love for the realization of his mad dreams.

EVA: George no longer loves me? Yet, I still love him. I will always love him. Always, you hear!

(Volsius enters)

DOCTOR OX: (beside himself) Shut up! Shut up! Beware of making me desperate. Stop trying to torture my soul.

VOLSIUS: Aren't you yourself trying to torture hers?

DOCTOR OX: Who dares to speak to me in this manner?

VOLSIUS: (approaching) I.

DOCTOR OX: We are no longer aboard your ship, Captain Nemo. And you are no longer all powerful here. Take care!

VOLSIUS: I warn you, sir, I am not easy to intimidate.

DOCTOR OX: What's that to me? And who asked for your intervention?

EVA: It's I, I who invoke it.

VOLSIUS: (to Eva) And it won't be in vain.

DOCTOR OX: Captain Nemo intends to contend against me—?

VOLSIUS: I intend to snatch from your hands he who your cursed science is leading from an intermittent delirium which obsesses him, to a decisive and terrible madness. I intend to do it, and I will find in your very self a weapon against you.

THE VOYAGE THROUGH THE IMPOSSIBLE, BY JULES VERNE * 101

DOCTOR OX: A weapon! In me? A weapon against me?

VOLSIUS: You love this young girl and the love which consumes your soul will be your punishment. It will fight for us.

DOCTOR OX: My love!

VOLSIUS: God said to the serpent: woman will crush your head under her heel. And as for me, I say to you: this woman will break your pride beneath her disdain. This weapon will crush your scorn and your hate.

DOCTOR OX: We shall see about that.

VOLSIUS: We shall see.

(Acclamations off)

DOCTOR OX: While waiting, Listen! It's the people of Atlantis who acclaim him; who are leading him to the throne where love and glory await him together.

EVA: Love?

DOCTOR OX: Yes, yes. The most beautiful of the daughters of this country; the descendant of King Atlas is destined for him.

EVA: My God!

DOCTOR OX: And this time he will no longer be only

forgetful. This will be betrayal. Your George will love another.

EVA: No, no. It's impossible.

(A huge cortège of all the court of the King of Atlantis enters; warriors and lords surrounding the new king. George, dressed in a royal costume takes his place on the bottom steps of a throne raised at the back in the midst of music and the acclamations of the people)

ALL: Halleluah! Halleluah!

GEORGE: People of Atlantis, I accept the crown of this immense realm. And its power shall not diminish under the reign of Hatteras!

ALL: Long live Hatteras!

(The cortège accompanying Princes Celena enters. Electra advances toward the princess and escorts her to the bottom steps of George's throne.)

ELECTRA: And now, King—here's Princess Celena who will become through you our queen.

ALL: Halleluah! For Celena.

(The Princess goes to take her place beside George.)

EVA: (hurling forward) His wife! No, no, that's impossible. George! George! Do you no longer remember the past, your oaths, our loves? George, do you want me to die at your feet?

GEORGE: (low) Eva, you will share my throne, my power.

EVA: But this throne is ephemera; this power chimerical.

GEORGE: What do you say?

EVA: Return to reality.

DOCTOR OX: The reality, George Hatteras, is all that you see. It's all that surrounds you. It's your glory, already great, which will soon be more dazzling still.

GEORGE: Speak. Explain yourself.

EVA: Don't listen to him George. Don't listen to him.

DOCTOR OX: I promised in your name to your new subjects that the work of Atlantis would be accomplished by you.

EVA: What did you dare say?

DOCTOR OX: I said—I said to the people of Atlantis that their king would realize the great attempt previously aborted. They say Atlas was struck by lightning. But to your Jupiter he will oppose a new thunder created by the genius of man. And, borne by this thunder he will hurl into space bronze or steel; he will cross the universe and he'll rise even to the celestial day!

GEORGE: (delirious) Yes! That's the way it will be done.

EVA: Alas! All is lost!

ALL: Glory to him! Glory to the son of Hatteras!

VOLSIUS: Don't despair. The dream will soon evaporate and with reality his reason will return. But for the last time, perhaps—

GEORGE: After the bowels of the Earth and the depth of the Ocean, space, infinity, Heaven—

(Some knights lead in a horse; George and the horse are raised in the air on a richly mounted shield. amidst fanfares.)

ALL: Halleluah! Halleluah!

CURTAIN

ACT III

SCENE XIV

THE GUN CLUB

(A large hall in the Gun Club in the United States. Trophies. Columns formed by cannons supported by mortars. Garlands of bombs; necklaces of projectiles; from the walls garlands of shells are suspended. To the right, the desk of the President of the club. In front, benches occupied by members of the association. It is day. President Barbicane is seated at his desk on which are arranged revolvers that serve as his ringer to reestablish order, and from time to time he fires shots in the air.)

(At rise, the tumult of the assembly is complete.)

FIRST GROUP: Yes! Yes! yes!

SECOND GROUP: No! no! no!

BARBICANE: My dear colleagues—

FIRST GROUP: To the devil with the proposition.

SECOND GROUP: And those who proposed it!

BARBICANE: A little silence if you please.

FIRST GROUP: Yes! Yes! Yes!

SECOND GROUP: No! no! no!

AN USHER: Silence gentlemen.

(Barbicane fires a pistol.)

MASTON: Let President Barbicane speak! What a president, gentlemen, what a president!

BARBICANE: Gentlemen, the question is very simple and it would already have been resolved if you were less noisy.

FIRST MEMBER: But we are artillery men in the Gun Club.

MASTON: And what artillery men, gentlemen! Artillery men and Americans.

FIRST MEMBER: And because of this double title we have double the right to be noisy.

FIRST GROUP: Yes, yes, yes!

SECOND GROUP: No, no, no!

BARBICANE: Gentlemen, I think you are going too far.

FIRST MEMBER: An artilleryman can never go too far.

MASTON: Any more than his shell.

BARBICANE: Gentlemen!

FIRST GROUP: Yes, yes, yes!

SECOND GROUP: No, no, no.

(Barbicane fires again.)

USHER: Silence, gentlemen.

(Silence is reestablished.)

BARBICANE: Gentlemen, you recall in what primitive condition our first experiment was conducted. A gigantic cannon, a Columbiad, was erected on the soil of Florida. A projectile was inserted. Three travelers took their place. My friend Captain Nicholl….

MASTON: What a Captain, gentlemen, what a captain!

BARBICANE: Our friend, Ardan, the French interpreter.

MASTON: What a Frenchman, gentleman, what a Frenchman!

BARBICANE: And me, your President.

MASTON: What a president.

BARBICANE: But due to an error in aiming the goal was not achieved and our projectile only went around the Moon and returned to fall into the Pacific. Now, the Columbiad is still there. It suffices to reload it. Is it agreed to renew the experiment and to send a second projectile towards the Moon, in a way to reach it this time?

FIRST GROUP: Yes, yes, yes.

SECOND GROUP: No, no, no.

BARBICANE: I think I understand you to say yes?

SECOND GROUP: No, no, no.

BARBICANE: At least it's not no.

SECOND GROUP: Yes, yes, yes.

FIRST AND SECOND GROUP No, no, no! Yes! Yes! Yes!

(General tumult; Barbicane fires again.)

USHER: Silence, gentlemen.

MASTON: It is necessary for the honor of the club that the experiment be renewed.

ALL: Voice vote! Voice vote!

MASTON: (to his neighbor) I forbid you to vote against the proposition.

FIRST MEMBER: I forbid you to vote for—

MASTON: (carried away) You'll give me satisfaction!

FIRST MEMBER: How can you expect me to give you something you've never had?

MASTON: Sir!

FIRST MEMBER: Sir!

BARBICANE: Gentlemen, ORDER! This is not the Congress! What the Devil!

FIRST MEMBER Your choice of weapons?

MASTON: Yours?

FIRST MEMBER: Repeating rifle.

MASTON: Gatling gun!

FIRST MEMBER: In an hour.

MASTON: Immediately!

BARBICANE: Gentlemen.

FIRST MEMBER: At fifteen paces.

MASTON: Ten!

FIRST MEMBER Five paces!

MASTON: Foot to foot.

FIRST MEMBER: Let's go outside.

MASTON: No—we'll fight here.

FIRST GROUP: Yes, yes, yes—

SECOND GROUP: No, no, no.

(Maston and the First Member rush at each other.)

BARBICANE: Separate them!

FIRST GROUP: Charge for Maston!

SECOND GROUP: Charge against Maston.

(The members of the club charge each other to support their partisans. President Barbicane vainly fires off several rounds.)

USHER: Silence, gentlemen.

(A second usher enters in the midst of the disorder and gives a letter to President Barbicane.)

BARBICANE: If I make this proposal to you, it's because I just received this here letter from the celebrated Doctor Ox.

ALL: The Celebrated Doctor Ox.

MASTON: What a Doctor, gentlemen, what a Doctor!

A MEMBER: And what's the letter say?

ALL: Listen! Listen!

BARBICANE: (reading) Illustrious President: Doctor Ox and his young companion George Hatteras have just arrived in this town and they ask to make a proposal to the members of The Gun Club which is of a nature to keenly interest them.

MASTON: A proposal.

BARBICANE: I think we ought to hear it. Is Doctor Ox there?

USHER: He's ready to present himself before the members of The Gun Club.

BARBICANE: (then, everybody) Show him in!

(Enter George and Doctor Ox.)

BARBICANE: Be welcome, illustrious Doctor Ox—

MASTON: (then, ALL) Honor to Doctor Ox.

DOCTOR OX: Allow me, first of all, gentlemen to present to you my young companion, George Hatteras son of the Glorious Captain Hatteras.

MASTON: Honor to the son of Captain Hatteras.

ALL: Honor! Honor!

GEORGE: Before honoring me with your acclamations gentlemen, first know what I have done and what I intend still to accomplish.

ALL: Speak!

DOCTOR OX: What he has done you will soon learn; and what he intends to attempt to do—to conquer the immense domain of space. He comes to ask you to facilitate his task.

GEORGE: Yes, I aspire to leave this earth that I have investigated to its profoundest depths. And it is outside our globe that I intend to place my foot into infinity.

BARBICANE: You can count on our cooperation.

DOCTOR OX: Here's the proposal we've come to communicate to you.

MASTON: (shouting) Silence, gentlemen, silence.

BARBICANE: But no one is speaking but you, Mr. Maston.

MASTON: Ah! Well then—I was addressing myself.

DOCTOR OX: Gentlemen, after this first experiment which brought clouds of glory to America, you had no thought of destroying the gigantic Columbiad whose shell raised itself more than a hundred thousand leagues into the air. And we ask you to renew the experiment, adjusting the trajectory this time in a way so as not to fail in its objective. (whispering by members of the club)

GEORGE: Well? Do you accept, gentlemen? Would you, in my person, conquer this satellite of the earth? The most audacious among you have not yet made the trip. Will you allow me, in this way, at last, to complete the third stage of my voyage through the impossible?

ALL: Yes! Yes.

DOCTOR OX: By accepting our proposal you will have once more demonstrated that nothing is impossible in this world.

MASTON: The word is not American.

GEORGE: Nor English.

VOLSIUS: (appearing disguised as Ardan) Nor French, gentlemen.

MASTON: Ardan. Our friend, Ardan.

ALL: Hurrah! For Ardan!

BARBICANE: My brave companion. (leaving his desk to shake hands with Ardan as all the members surround him)

VOLSIUS: Yes, it is I, my friends! Michel Ardan. The "Labrador" disembarked me just now. I learned that the Gun Club was in session and my first visit is to you.

MASTON: What a man! Even though he is a Frenchman.

BARBICANE: The French are a great nation, gentlemen, and they lack only one thing to become the first nation in the world.

MASTON: Yes. One alone.

VOLSIUS: Which is?

MASTON: Being American.

VOLSIUS: Thanks!

BARBICANER: My dear companion you come just in time. Our first attempt has found imitators.

VOLSIUS: Imitators! What, there exist under the canopy of heaven, madmen more mad than we have been?

MASTON: Mad?

DOCTOR OX: I don't recognize the language of the audacious Ardan.

VOLSIUS: You are saying, sir?

BARBICANE: Doctor Ox, and his young companion, George Hatteras

GEORGE: —have resolved, sir, to take possession of a world which escaped you.

VOLSIUS: How's that, young man! Why, make yourself at home! The Moon belongs to the first occupant! And then what? What will you do with the Moon?

GEORGE: We will do with it—

MASTON: A gift to the United States. It will be the next state in the Union!

ALL: Yes, yes!

VOLSIUS: The Moon? Why, it's an old star—finished, old-fashioned, and even a little ridiculous. She's had her day, this old Astarte, mummified sister of radiant Apollo. They'll laugh at your voyage, and on your return you will hear your fellow creatures saying to you, "Did you really see the Moon, my little boy?"

DOCTOR OX: Is it indeed the celebrated Ardan who

speaks this way?

VOLSIUS: And besides, one day all the world will go to the Moon and further still. Aerial trains will be plowing the air. Instead of wagons on rails we will place projectiles on them and hurl them into space. Trains to all the planets. Express to Mercury, Jupiter, Uranus and Neptune! It will soon be only the outskirts of the Earth, and they'll pass by it every Sunday as the Parisians go to Chatou or even Vesinet!

MASTON: Well said, friend Ardan.

VOLSIUS: Believe me then, George Hatteras. Abandon this project and return quietly home.

GRORGE: I should renounce leaving this Earth!

VOLSIUS: Oh—you will soon leave it; all too soon, my dear fellow.

DOCTOR OX: Ah! Mr. Ardan, you think that the Moon is unworthy of being explored by us?

VOLSIUS: That's my opinion, Doctor Ox:

DOCTOR OX: Well, you've convinced me.

GEORGE: Is it possible?

DOCTOR OX: Yes, yes, we must renounce this humble planet, this cold satellite of Earth. We must hurl ourselves toward a more distant, more noble end.

VOLSIUS AND ALL: What's he say?

GEORGE: Toward the Sun then?

DOCTOR OX: Further still.

GEORGE: Jupiter, Uranus?

DOCTOR OX: Further still! Much further! Out of our solar system.

GEORGE: (exalted) Ah, I understand, Doctor. Yes, yes. To go lose oneself in infinity, to run through the stars, to pass by those groups which light three or four suns gravitating under their influence. Ah! Admirable spectacle! Resplendent stars of a thousand diverse colors. Days made from all the colors, all the nuances of the rainbow that rise, radiant, on the horizon.

(Sounds of admiration.)

DOCTOR OX: It's there we will go, gentlemen. And your Columbiad which served to send a projectile to the Moon will indeed send that projectile millions of leagues.

BARBICANE: Yes! If you have the secret of a powder capable of giving it a sufficient thrust.

DOCTOR OX: I have discovered a propulsive force without limits and under its all powerful impetus our projectile will soon pass out of the solar system.

MASTON: Bravo, Doctor Ox! What a doctor, gentlemen, what a doctor!

BARBICANE: And to what point in space will you aim the Columbiad?

DOCTOR OX: Towards a new planet that the astronomers of Cambridge have just discovered. At the planet Altor!

ALL: Altor!

GEORGE: Yes! Altor! Altor!

BARBICANE: Honor to the audacious men who undertake this conquest.

ALL: Hurrah! Hurrah!

DOCTOR OX: (ironically) Well? What do you say about that, Mr. Ardan?

VOLSIUS: Me? Nothing, Doctor Ox.

DOCTOR OX: Not a word of blame or criticism for this audacious attempt by Hatteras?

VOLSIUS: Why would I blame him? I also intend to leave with him.

ALL: Ah!

DOCTOR OX: What? You pretend?

VOLSIUS: To become your companion if you will permit it, Hatteras?

GEORGE: Yes, surely. You will leave with us. You will share our glory.

DOCTOR OX: (aside) We'll see about that!

VOLSIUS: We will meet again in Florida, gentlemen at the very foot of the Columbiad.

BARBICANE: We will all be there!

ALL: Hurrah! Hurrah! Hurrah!

BLACKOUT/CURTAIN

SCENE XV

THE CANNON SHOT

(The stage represents a plain in Florida in the South of the United States. A gigantic cannon of which we see only the lower part is poised erect in its gun carriage. At the back, a whole city, with its clocks, its houses and its trees. Broad daylight.)

MASTON: Gentlemen, it's here I have the responsibility

to escort you.

TARTELET: Pardon! To whom have we the honor of speaking?

MASTON: Maston. Pure-blooded American.

VALDEMAR: Ah, ah. You hear, Tartelet? This gentleman is a pure blood.

MASTON: American—old rock.

VALDEMAR: This gentleman is old rock.

MASTON: American! Old stump.

VALDEMAR: This gentleman is an old stump.

TARTELET: That's apparent.

MASTON: Member of the Gun Club. I've invented a marvelous cannon.

TARTELET: Really.

MASTON: A cannon which goes up to 1,250 feet over the target one wishes to hit.

VALDEMAR: (reaching for his hand) What precision.

TARTELET: It's admirable.

MASTON: I've conceived of another whose shell can knock down eight hundred men and 200 horses at the same time.

TARTEKLET: Four men per horse.

VALDEMAR: Like the son of Aymon.

MASTON: I wanted to make a test of it; the horses made no objection, but the men were mulishly unwilling.

TARTELET: Well, I understand that.

VALDEMAR: Ah! if you employed the other cannon which overshot the target by 1,250 feet, the horses would still have nothing to say, but perhaps the men would have consented more willingly.

TARTELET: But why did you bring us here, sir?

MASTON: Your companion, Mr. George Hatteras, begs you to wait for him here if you are still determined to follow him on his new journey.

TARTELET: Sir, we are very determined.

VALDEMAR: Certainly. But where are we going?

MASTON: To the Altorians.

VALDEMAR: Don't know the Altorians.

TARTELET: What part of the Earth do they live in?

MASTON: Why, no part.

VALDEMAR: What do you mean no part?

MASTON: Certainly. Altor is a recently discovered planet and that's where you are going.

VALDEMAR: Excuse me, excuse me. That's where we are going? And by what means if you please?

TARTELET: Yes. By what method of locomotion?

MASTON: (pointing to the huge cannon) The means? There it is.

VALDEMAR: (terrified) That? Come on! Why, it's—

TARTELET: It's a cannon.

VALDEMAR: An immense cannon.

MASTON: It's a Columbiad.

VALDEMAR AND TARTELET: A Columbiad?

MASTON: Provided with a wagon projectile that, hurled by several thousand kilos of picrate explosives will lead you straight to the planet Altor.

VALDEMAR: And you think that I'm going to get into

that? Me and my seventeen million dollar diamond! Ah, no indeed. Ah, no indeed!

MASTON: As you please.

VALDEMAR: Are you going to canonize yourself, Tartelet?

TARTELET: (calmly) Me? That depends.

VALDEMAR: It depends on what?

TARTELET: (to Maston) Miss Eva must be going, too?

MASTON: Doubtless. She's said nothing will separate her from her friends.

TARTELET: Well, as for me, nothing will separate me from her.

VALDEMAR: Why, it's madness, Tartelet.

TARTELET: You're probably right, Valdemar, but when I arrived at the home of this young girl's grandmother, I was really poor and really abandoned. I was famished. And those two excellent women greeted me, not as a beggar, but as a friend. That's why I followed Miss Eva when she left. And today, when new danger arises before her greater perhaps than all the others am I to abandon her and return calmly to her grandmother and say "I left your daughter, Madam; the energy that love gave to that child, gratitude was unable to inspire in a man!"

Come on! I wouldn't have the courage to be so cowardly as that.

VALDEMAR: (moved) Well, me neither! And I won't be separated from you, Tartelet. It's fine, very fine, what you just said, Tartelet. And you won't have to wait to install yourself in my mansion. It will be a palace. My friendship, my table, my purse, and a little piece of my diamond—all that is yours, Tartelet. (embracing him and kissing him on the cheek)

MASTON: Then you'll be on the voyage—both of you?

VALDEMAR: (with energy) Yes, both of us. And I wish we were already parted; I wish we were already back.

TARTELET: What time is the departure?

MASTON: Forty-two minutes past noon by my chronometer.

VALDEMAR: Ah! Ah! By the way, before leaving, I am going to see if my reply has arrived. Perhaps they forgot to bring it to me here.

TARTELET: What reply?

VALDEMAR: I expedited another dispatch to the cruel Babichok, to tell her all that I've done, and to inform her of all I am going to do—again, so she'll really know. Ah, what a hero she's scorned. What a hero. Excuse me, gentlemen. (he leaves as George and Doctor

Ox arrive)

GEORGE: Here—it's here.

DOCTOR OX: This is the place on the terrestrial globe that your foot will tread on for the last time.

MASTON: And here's the gigantic cannon which will give us the first thrust towards infinity.

DOCTOR OX: Towards a world more ancient than ours. And whose inhabitants have perhaps invented all that we will invent one day.

GEORGE: In such a way that, having been thrown back into the past, we are going to hurl ourselves toward the future.

TARTELET: But how will we get into the inside of this cannon?

MASTON: You are going to know.

(Maston releases a spring and the breach of the cannon opens to reveal a projectile which then opens and whose interior is furnished like a cabin.)

MASTON: You see your wagon-projectile is furnished like a first class compartment.

GEORGE: Indeed, but isn't the departure time soon? Hurry up. (low to Doctor Ox) I don't want Eva to confront any new dangers.

DOCTOR OX: Don't be concerned; she won't leave.

(Volsius, Barbicane, and all the members of the Gun Club enter along with a crowd of spectators.)

BARBICANE: Ah—we are coming to address a last farewell to you, gentlemen. All the preparations are finished, Maston?

MASTON: All!

(Enter an employee of the telegraph.)

TARTELET: Ah. The employee of the telegraph. (to Employee) Doubtless you are seeking Mr. Valdemar?

EMPLOYEE: Yes, sir.

TARTELET: You've got a dispatch for him? Give it to me; I'll take it to him. (taking it and putting it in his pocket)

MASTON: Thirty-nine minutes past noon.

GEORGE: Let's depart.

DOCTOR OX: Yes. Let's depart! Let's depart.

BARBICANE: Goodbye, then, my friends. Goodbye. We will accompany you with our hurrahs.

ALL: Hurrah! Hurrah! (acclamations from all sides.)

GEORGE: To infinity! To infinity!

VALDEMAR: (running up) Whew! I've got here in time, I think.

TARTELET: Hurry up then, Valdemar, we were going to leave without you.

VASLDEMAR: Without me!

TARTELET: Gentlemen, travelers to Altor—into the cannon.

VALDEMAR: Into the cannon.

TARTELET: Ah! My God—and Miss Eva?

VALDEMAR: And Mr. Ardan?

VOLSIUS: (entering with Eva) Here we are, gentlemen. Miss begged me to accompany her.

GEORGE: Eva.

DOCTOR OX: Silence. They won't depart.

MASTON: At forty-two minutes past noon I will give the signal.

(George and Ox enter the projectile followed by Tartelet

and Valdemar.)

VOLSIUS: Come, Eva!

EVA: Yes, yes! Come!

(Both approach the cannon, but as they are about to enter the hatch is locked from within,)

EVA: Great God.

VOLSIUS: Ah, Doctor, you intend to leave without us. (to Eva) Don't be upset, my child. We will get to the planet Altor before them.

MASTON'S VOICE: Forty-two past noon. FIRE!

(The detonation can be heard and a strong recoil motion of the Columbiad reveals the entire countryside at the back. The spectators are grouped around the cannon waving their handkerchiefs and making the air vibrate with their shouting.)

ALL: Hurrah! Hurrah!

BLCKOUT /curtain

SCENE XVI

THE PLANET ALTOR

(A public place on the planet Altor. In the distance in silhouette, the outline of a city which appears to be built of gold. To the right, the façade of a habitation whose walls are encrusted with precious stone. Several Altorians are present.)

FIRST ALTORIAN: I repeat that an enormous meteor just fell an instant ago.

SECOND ALTORIAN: As for me, I was able to follow its fall; and, piercing the stratums of air, it produced a terrifying whistle.

FIRST ALTORIAN: We've got to take it to the museum; it's never had the like.

ALL: Yes! Yes!

FIRST ALTORIAN: Look, look. An opening just appeared in the meteor.

SECOND ALTORIAN: Two men are coming out.

FIRST ALTORIAN: Three, four men.

VALDEMAR: (walking, but lifting his feet very high) What a fancy strut I've got here.

TARTELET: (same action) Me, too. What a strange walk.

VALDEMAR: My feet don't cling to the Earth.

TARTELET: Nor mine.

VALDEMAR: (to the Altorians) Gentlemen. I am really honored. The planet Altor, if you please.

FIRST ALTORIAN: This is it.

VALDEMAR: Ah! I'm not sorry to get here. (calling) Hey! Down there—my brave companions!

TARTELET: They're going to come. They are examining this singular country.

VALDEMAR: Ah! We are on the planet Altor.

FIRST ALTORIAN: Yes! And where are you from?

TARTELET: From Earth.

ALL THE ALTORIANS: From Earth?

VALDEMAR: But what's that city that we notice down there? (going to the back)

FIRST ALTORIAN: That's our capital.

TARTELET: One would say it's built completely of gold.

VALDEMAR: The Devil. That's worth the trip.

TARTELET: And will you indeed escort us there?

FIRST ALTORIAN: Why, of course. We even ask your permission to present you to the Academy of Sciences.

TARTELET: To the Academy of Sciences?

FIRST ALTORIAN: And then put you in the Museum of Natural History.

VALDEMAR: Stuffed?

SECOND ALTORIAN: Oh, no. Embalmed.

TARTELET: Embalmed. I protest.

FIRST ALTORIAN: Oh, much later. Only when you are deceased.

VALDEMAR: You are indeed good, sir.

TARTELET: Lead us there. We are ready to follow you.

VALDEMAR: Damn! Why the city is far away. Couldn't we rest a little before starting on our way?

FIRST ALTORIAN: Here's the dwelling of a scientist, newly arrived with his daughter from regions most distant from Altor. (pointing to the dwelling at the right) He won't refuse you entry to his cottage.

TARTELET: A cottage. This? With walls encrusted with expensive gems?

VALDEMAR: And a humble cottage of gold. Why, we are but beggars here. My diamond is of no value. See it. (taking it from his pocket)

FIRST ALTORIAN: You can pick up bigger and more beautiful diamonds than that anywhere

VALDEMAR: Ah! Bah!

FIRST ALTORIAN: (looking at it) We wouldn't even use that to pave our streets.

VALDEMAR: It's not worth a simple paving stone. Then I am ruined. And I shan't keep it any longer. Ah, indeed, no! (throws it) Ah! Indeed, no!

(Volsius appears in the doorway of the "cottage" dressed as an Altorian)

VOLSIUS: Strangers.

TARTELET: Inhabitants of Earth, sir.

VOLSIUS: Earth. A planet of the twenty-fifth size which is lit by only one sun.

VALDEMAR: He finds one is not enough!

TARTELET: Pardon, sir. You have several here?

VOLSIUS: Here there are two suns and six moons that rise successively on the horizons of Altor.

TARTELET: Two suns?

VALDEMAR: Six moons? So that if one of the six moons

disappears.

TARTELET: You still have five remaining. (to Volsius) You seem well acquainted with the planet we just left!

VOLSIUS: Yes, we know it. For the last 200 thousand years that our generations have succeeded each other, progress here has reached in three things the highest degree and our telescope whose magnification is so to speak, limitless, allows us to view your Earth as if it were less than a league away.

TARTELET: That's admirable.

VOLSIUS: But there are certain points about which our science would like to be informed. What sort of city is it where one notices a hill that dominates it, a winding river which crosses it, monuments, squares, and people everywhere, lots of people, bustling about in the fog during winter and the dust during summer?

TARTELET: (aside) A city that they never water. That must be Paris.

VOLSIUS: We've distinctly noticed a great square with a bridge at one end, and facing this bridge, a sort of Palace before which assemble a crowd of men of affaires, who talk a lot but never listen.

VALDEMAR: I know that country. I've gone there. The Bridge is called the Bridge of Concorde and the palace which is at the end, The Palace of Discor—no, the

Chamber of Deputies.

TARTELET: Yes, it's the Palace of the Legislative Body (aside) What am I going to do here?

VOLSIUS: What is done in that Palace?

VALDEMAR: What do they do there? They defeat ministries.

VOLSIUS: It seems also that from time to time they squabble a lot in that city. They fight; then they embrace; then they fight anew and then they embrace again.

TARTELET: There can be no more doubt. That's the capital of our beautiful France.

VALDEMAR: Paris—ate beef there, etc.

VOLSIUS: Your country then is not easy to govern?

TARTELET: And yours, sir?

VOLSIUS: Ours is different. It governs itself, by itself.

TARTELET: By itself?

VOLSIUS: Yes; we've tried all forms of government over several thousand years. Absolute monarchy overthrown by constitutional monarchy. Constitutional monarchy overthrown by Republican government.

TARTELET: And the republic itself?

VOLSIUS: Overthrown by Republicans.

TARTELET: And finally you arrived at?

VOLSIUS: At having no government at all.

VALDEMAR: And that works?

VOLSIUS: That works to perfection. That works so much better. For through Progress the whole world has become knowledgeable. The shoemakers write verse and the butchers practice anatomy. We lack workers and we will be forced to come to decree: obligatory ignorance.

TARTELET: Mandatory ignorance?

VOLSIUS: What's more, sir, we have over population which is becoming very embarrassing. For it increases every day and no one dies here except after two or three hundred years of existence.

VALDEMAR: You live for 300 years here?

VOLSIUS: Yes, sir.

VALDEMAR: Then you don't have doctors?

VOLSIUS: We imprudently suppressed them! Later we wanted to create them anew, but the new ones hadn't time to really learn medicine which causes them to cure those who are ill.

VALDEMAR: Pardon. A bit of information, if you please. Since coming here I feel myself as light as a feather. I walk like a butterfly.

TARTELET: And me, too. I lift my feet so high it seems to me I have the gait of a rooster.

VALDEMAR: Or of a Turkey! (they walk raising their legs)

VOLSIUS: It's all quite simple, gentlemen. You make an effort to act and walk on this planet equal to that you made on yours.

TARTELET AND VALDEMAR: Indeed, yes.

VOLSIUS: And as the mass of Altor is twenty times smaller than that of Earth, the attraction toward the center is much weaker; and your muscular strength seems increased a hundredfold.

TARTELET: Ah, Good. Right.

VALDEMAR: Mighty fine! I didn't understand at all.

TARTELET: So, if I were to give dancing lessons here?

VOLSIUS: You would see your students rise to abnormal heights.

TARTELET: And if I were to try a caper?

VOLSIUS: (laughing) You might find yourself flying.

VALDEMAR: Don't do anything stupid. Don't do any capering, Tartelet.

VOLSIUS: But they told me four strangers, and—

TARTELET: Our traveling companions are here—nearby! Busy looking at the great works—

VOLSIUS: A gigantic work undertaken by our engineers.

GEORGE: (coming up) Yes, yes. Gigantic indeed! Colossal ports and immense locks seem destined to give passage to waves from an ocean that is going to hurl itself out of the bed nature created for it.

VOLSIUS: You are not mistaken; that's indeed what it is all about, gentlemen.

GEORGE: But the reason? The purpose?

DOCTOR OX: (who has come up with George) This world we've just reached counts its existence in millions of years. It has drained the soil to nourish its population which has become innumerable. It has drained its quarries in order to house them; it has excavated bottomless mines to satisfy the needs of industry and civilization—with the result that in all parts immense trenches riddle this planet to its profoundest depths.

VALDEMAR: Why, it's not safe here.

VOLSIUS: No! Because the central core, no longer contained by a shell sufficiently solid, threatens to escape.

DOCTOR OX: And millions of craters may open from one moment to the next.

TARTELET: Well! We've arrived at a nice time!

VALDEMAR: (to Volsius) Pardon, sir. How to get to Copenhagen, if you please?

VOLSIUS: Rest easy. Our scientists say they have found the means for the time being to ward off the danger of dying by famine or fire.

GEORGE: And the way is—?

DOCTOR OX: (ironically) First of all to cultivate these vast plains so as to recover the sea, they want to spread it through these immense cavities I just spoke of that reach the planet's center.

VOLSIUS: Where it will put out the fire that threatens to erupt.

GEORGE: Do they dare accomplish this incomparable work?

DOCTOR OX: This formidable madness?

GEORGE: It's a marvelous conception. I wish to take part in its implementation.

VOLSIUS: Nothing could be easier. For today is actually when the opening of these dams will take place. Come, gentlemen, before taking you to our capital, my daughter and I will do you the honors of our house. (George and Doctor Ox head toward the dwelling, followed by Volsius)

TARTELET: (as he pulls out his handkerchief, he lets a paper fall) Come on! My, my. What's that? Ah! The dispatch they gave me on earth for Valdemar that I forgot to give him. Hey, Valdemar! Valdemar! (Valdemar is about to follow the others into the house when Tartelet grabs him by the arm)

VALDEMAR: Mr. Tartelet!

TARTELET: My friend, just as we were going to take our place in the Columbiad, a dispatch arrived for you.

VALDEMAR: And this dispatch?

TARTELET: You weren't there yet; they gave it to me. And my word, I confess to you, I had forgotten it in my pocket.

VALDEMAR: Ah. Great God. A response. A response from Miss Babichok. Why, gimme, gimme.

TARTELET: Here it is.

VALDEMAR: (reading) "Terrible occurrence. At our wedding banquet your cousin Finderup swallowed a fish bone which choked him." (sadly) Dead. He's dead—that poor Finderup is dead—(smiling) During the wedding banquet. Tsk! tsk! tsk! Between noon and one o'clock Babichok is a widow, my friend—the very day of her marriage. Eh! Tsk! tsk! And between noon and one o'clock Ah! ah! ah!

TARTELET: Finish the dispatch.

VALDEMAR: Yes, yes, I'm finishing. (very sadly) Cousin Finderup swallowed a bone. Cousin Finderup choked to death! (gaily) "Return quickly. (with feeling) Who cares if you are a bit fat so long as the diamond is huge." Oh, she's sweet, she's delicate, she's tender.

TARTELET: Very tender. Yes.

VALDEMAR: Babichok! Darling Babichok! She hopes for me, she's waiting for me. Quick! Quick! I am rushing to rejoin her. Horses, a carriage, a train.

TARTELET: You want to cross Space, Infinity, in a carriage, in a train?

VALDEMAR: That's right. I am no longer thinking straight. What? You deliver this dispatch to me here?

TARTELET: Alas, yes.

VALDEMAR: When down there, at the moment it came, I

was only 1,500 leagues from Babichok!

TARTELET: What do you want? It's a small omission.

VALDEMAR: He calls this a small omission! When Babichok is waiting for me; when she is free, a widow—choked to death, meaning him, Finderup. Why do you know, sir, I have the right to hold you responsible for whatever may happen?

TARTELET: Responsible? Me! Come on!

VALDEMAR: (enraged) If she marries another one—do you understand, will you undertake to choke him to death?

TARTELET: Mr. Valdemar. I advise you to speak to me in a more proper tone or else!

VALDEMAR: Or else! What? What? What?

TARTELET: Mr. Valdemar, take care!

VALDEMAR: You take care yourself. Don't forget that on this planet my strength is increased tenfold.

TARTELET: Mine too, I suppose. And the proof is—there! So much the worse if it is. (giving Valdemar a kick in the derrière which lifts him two feet off the ground)

VALDEMAR: Huh? What's that mean?

TARTELET: (laughing) Ha, ha, ha. The lack of gravity. Feet out, sir, feet out!

VALDEMAR: Ah! Rogue! (kicks him in turn)

TARTELET: (rising to the same height) Ah! (falling back)

VALDEMAR: Lack of gravity, sir, lack of gravity. Ah! Hush! People are coming!

EVA: (entering in Altorian dress from the dwelling) My father's house is open to you.

TARTELET: Your father's house? Ah, yes. Pardon, miss.

EVA: Your friends are awaiting you.

VALDEMAR: We are going to find them.

TARTELET: (threateningly) Whenever you like, sir (they meet each other at the door)

VALDEMAR: (amiably) After you!

TARTELET: (amiably also) Go ahead in!

VALDEMAR: I won't do anything.

TARTELET: If you insist. (they enter at the same time)

EVA: (dreamily) My mysterious protector tells me that soon George's reason will be reborn. But possibly for the last time. And doubtless it is here that our cruel enemy will make him submit to a test. One that will ruin him without hope. Oh! I don't want to remain a stranger to his sight any longer. It's to share his perils that I followed him. I will make him recognize me. But only him. Vainly has Doctor Ox's glance rested on me. As for him, he hasn't recognized me.

DOCTOR OX: There she is; it's really her!

EVA: Get out! Him!

DOCTOR OX: A single moment, I beg you.

EVA: My father's waiting for me, excuse me.

DOCTOR OX: The man in there is not your father and I recognize you.

EVA: As for me, I don't recognize you.

DOCTOR OX: I am, unaware through what power, what miracle has led you here. But you are Eva and you know that I—

EVA: I don't know you, I tell you!

DOCTOR OX: Well, so be it. I am mistaken and truly, I am not sorry to be. It would have been bad of me to force that young girl I was speaking to you about to witness what's going to happen here.

EVA: What's going to happen here!

DOCTOR OX: It would have been bad of me, I say, for her to be witness, not only to the dementia, but also the death of her fiancé.

EVA: (forgetting herself) He's going to die! George!

DOCTOR OX: (forcefully) You see perfectly well I wasn't mistaken.

EVA: Well yes; I gave myself away. Yes, I am Eva. But what do you expect from this confession you've torn from me? What more do you want from me?

DOCTOR OX: For one last time, I want to attempt to move you and soften your heart.

EVA: And has your heart softened? Have you ceased to persecute me?

DOCTOR OX: It's not you! It's him; him, my detested rival!

EVA: But he's my whole life.

DOCTOR OX: Don't tell me that!

EVA: He's all my soul.

DOCTOR OX: Shut up.

EVA: He's all my happiness; all my love.

DOCTOR OX: (forceful) Enough! Enough, I tell you!

EVA: And by butchering him you intend to get to me! Ah, you murder me and you want me to love you! Well, know this: as much as you resent George, whom I adore—I resent you. You hate him; I hate you.

DOCTOR OX: (beside himself) Eva! But what can I do? Her voice, quivering with rage and hate echoes to the depths of my soul! Ah, perhaps I could resign myself to the misery of not being loved by you. But to be hated? Never! Oh, wretch that I am; I've discovered the most powerful secrets of nature; I've acquired a superhuman science. Only to be miserably annihilated at the feet of a child. Ah, Captain Nemo indeed said that it would be in my own heart that weapons would be found against me. Well, yes, my pride is vanquished; yes my heart is broken. I beg you, I implore you. I am at your knees. Don't hate me, Eva! Don't hate me! (starts to pull at her and wants to grasp her hand)

EVA: (disengaging herself) Leave me alone! Leave me alone!

DOCTOR OX: I ask your mercy, Eva. Listen. Listen, do you want me to become your humble servant, your slave?

EVA: No!

DOCTOR OX: Well, wait, a thousand times more his—his slave. George's. Ah! That will be a great sacrifice and really excruciating, I swear to you. Never mind. Say a word, a word of compassion, of pity and I will do it. But don't hate me, don't hate me! Eva, don't hate me.

VOLSIUS: (coming from the dwelling) My daughter. (Eva slowly enters the house.)

DOCTOR OX: (starting to follow her, Volsius blocks his way. The two stare each other in the face) Eva—

VOLSIUS: That woman will crush your head under her heel.

DOCTOR OX: (watching Eva) That terrible curse. Is it coming across the ages to wear me down? No. I will triumph over this love. I will tear it from my heart. Ah! Ah! I cannot. I'll never be able to! That woman will crush me under her heel.

BLACKOUT/CURTAIN

SCENE XVII

THE END OF A WORLD

(An immense square bordered by a palace of unusual architecture. The walls are built of precious stone and marbles of the greatest beauty. Gold and silver appear everywhere. Shining light which has all the intensity of electric light.

A celebration in all its splendor is in progress. Full cups circulate between groups. Doctor Ox, George, Eva, Tartelet, Valdemar are present.)

BALLET

(A ballet of Altorians is abruptly interrupted at its height by a great noise of clocks and drums. George, followed by the other characters rushes into the midst of the dancers.)

GEORGE: The hour has struck and the gigantic work is being accomplished at this moment by the colossal gates that my hands opened. I've seen the ocean rushing into the gulf. I've seen it precipitate itself in the immense cataracts, and at the resounding noise of its fall. Prolonged, rolling subterranean thunder has responded. It seems as if this mass of fire is revolting against an enemy invasion. And the struggle between these elements singing in fury with great waves of suppressed steam. Sing, drink, dance: for you have accomplished an unprecedented work. It's a glorious triumph of man over nature. It's a magnificent spectacle that one would pay with one's life for.

VOLSIUS: (entering) Any you will soon pay for it with all your lives.

ALL: Ah!

EVA: What's he say!

DOCTOR OX: (with a strong and ironic voice) He is saying, poor fools that you are, that a terrible cataclysm is going to be produced, that you yourselves have provoked. The waters that you have precipitated into the central core won't extinguish it. Transformed into hoary steam it's going to blow up, and the debris of this planet is going to be strewn through space.

GEORGE: (delirious) Well, they will take us with them into other stellar worlds.

VOLSIUS: I tell you Altor has no more than a few moments of existence left.

GEORGE: (seizing a cup) Let's drink, friends, let's drink. And if death must strike us we will die in a last song of triumph.

EVA: We will die in a last prayer.

HALF THE INHABITANTS: Yes! Yes! Let's drink! Let's drink!

THE OTHER HALF: (kneeling) Let's pray.

(Dancing begins on one side, prayers on the other.)

SCENE XVIII

(A sudden terrifying explosion. All is hidden in the midst of smoke and flames. Everything is engulfed. There remain only a few shapeless ruins. The heaven is covered with clouds through which plow flashes of light and claps of thunder. All the characters are knocked down and seem dead. Doctor Ox and Volsius alone remain standing and glare at each other defiantly. A curtain of fog rises slowly towards the borders and little by little obscures the ruins and the characters.)

BLACKOUT/CURTAIN

SCENE XIX

CASTLE ANDERNAK

(The room in the castle just as it was in the first act. George is stretched out on a couch. Eva is keeling near him. Madame de Traventhal is near Eva. Tartelet is keeping back, a bit to the side. Volsius and Doctor Ox are by the patient's head.)

MADAME DE TRAVENTHAL Wretched child! Is this the way I must see him again!

EVA: My God, will he live? And if he lives will his reason remain forever lost?

TARTELET: (aside) Alas, I am much afraid of that.

VOLSIUS: Don't despair, child. Both of us, Doctor Ox and I will perhaps accomplish a double miracle.

DOCTOR OX: Both of us? What's he mean?

VOLSIUS: You are a powerful incarnation of that science

for which the body is everything, and that believes in nothing in the future. As for me, I am the humble servant of faith and I count as nothing our terrestrial mould. To return life to this body tell it: arise and walk. And I will strive to reawaken its reason and to return calm and strength to its immortal soul.

DOCTOR OX: Save him! Me!

EVA: You told me, my slave and his to be no longer hated. I renounce all hate. Save him!

(Doctor Ox pours several drops of a liqueur contained in a flask on George's lips.)

DOCTOR OX: And now, wait.

TARTELET: We'll wait! (seeing Valdemar enter) Valdemar—Hush! (signaling him not to make any noise)

VALDEMAR: (low, pulling Tartelet aside) Yes, it's me, Tartelet, and I am really happy and quite desperate at the same time.

TARTELET: What's the matter?

VALDEMAR: I've seen Babichok again. She was waiting for me, but she was also waiting for my diamond, and alas you know—(weeping) down there—in the planet— when it was valueless, I stupidly cast it away.

TARTELET: Yes, I retrieved it. I did!

VALDEMAR: (sadly) Ah, you retrieved it, Tartelet?

TARTELET: And I'm going to return it to you, Valdemar.

VALDEMAR: You're going to return it to me? Tartelet, my friend! We will offer it to Babichok together, the two of us. And we will marry her together—er, no.

DOCTOR OX: Look. His eyes are reopening; he's going to speak, he's getting up.

GEORGE: Ah.

DOCTOR OX: He's speaking.

GEORGE: (in total delirium) Where are we? Ah, the center of the Earth. Eva's going to die. She's escaped. Now the sea. Atlantis—and my kingdom, my triumph.

EVA: Alas! It's the same dementia.

VOLSIUS: My turn now. (going to the organ, he begins to play)

GEORGE: Altor! The planet Altor. A whole world was being destroyed. Some singing and drinking, others praying! (during these words, the decor has changed and represents a sort of aerial cathedral) They are praying and here's the celestial sanctuary. Ah, what a beneficent calm is spreading through my whole being. My face is refreshed and the veil which clouded my thinking is dissipating. Yes! Yes! I remember. I, I see, I rec-

ognize you all. (seizing Eva's hand) Eva—oh! Dearest
Eva! I love you. No more senseless dreams. Yours,
yours alone, forever!

VALDEMAR: Babichok's yours, yours, Valdemar!

TARTELET: (giving him the diamond) Your Valdemar.
And here's her diamond. (Valdemar throws himself into
Tartelet's arms)

CURTAIN

SCENE XX

APOTHEOSIS

(Volsius plays a sort of Hosanna. The cathedral is transformed again. At the back an entire "glory" appears sur-
rounded by angels. Doctor Ox, himself vanquished by the
sublimity of this vision, bows in his turn.)

FINAL CURTAIN

ABOUT FRANK J. MORLOCK

FRANK J. MORLOCK has written and translated many plays since retiring from the legal profession in 1992. His translations have also appeared on Project Gutenberg, the Alexandre Dumas Père web page, Literature in the Age of Napoléon, Infinite Artistries.com, and Munsey's (formerly Blackmask). In 2006 he received an award from the North American Jules Verne Society for his translations of Verne's plays. He lives and works in Maryland and México.

www.ingramcontent.com/pod-product-compliance
Lightning Source LLC
Chambersburg PA
CBHW020136180626
46810CB00004B/1594